"Sean Was My Son, Too"

Alan growled. "You make it seem like you're the only one allowed to grieve. Stop being so greedy, Kay."

"What do you mean?" she exploded.

"You cling to his memory like a miser. Are you trying to show the world that you loved him more than anyone else? Is that it? Are you trying to show that you loved him more than I did?" Suddenly he walked away from her. "I meant every word I ever said to you. I meant it when I asked you to marry me, when I said I wanted us to have a child, when I told you I believed times would be good for us again. And I mean it now when say I'm not going to spend the rest of my life waiting for you face up to reality."

ANTONIA SAXON

is a former actress whose first contact with publishing came as an editor. She now writes full-time, often making use of her travels to provide the backgrounds for her novels.

Dear Reader,

Silhouette Special Editions are an exciting new line of contemporary romances from Silhouette Books. Special Editions are written specifically for our readers who want a story with heightened romantic tension.

Special Editions have all the elements you've enjoyed in Silhouette Romances and *more*. These stories concentrate on romance in a longer, more realistic and sophisticated way, and they feature greater sensual detail.

I hope you enjoy this book and all the wonderful romances from Silhouette.

Karen Solem
Editor-in-Chief
Silhouette Books

ANTONIA SAXON

Above the Moon

Published by Silhouette Books New York
America's Publisher of Contemporary Romance

Silhouette Books by Antonia Saxon

Paradiso (SE #88)
Above the Moon (SE #141)

SILHOUETTE BOOKS, a Division of Simon & Schuster, Inc
1230 Avenue of the Americas, New York, N.Y. 10020

Distributed by Pocket Books

ISBN: 0-671-53641-9

First Silhouette Books printing January, 1984

10 9 8 7 6 5 4 3 2 1

Map by Ray Lungren

America's Publisher of Contemporary Romance

Printed in the U.S.A.

I would like to thank Dr. Virginia Pomerantz
and Dr. Gideon Panter of New York City
for their invaluable information and assistance.

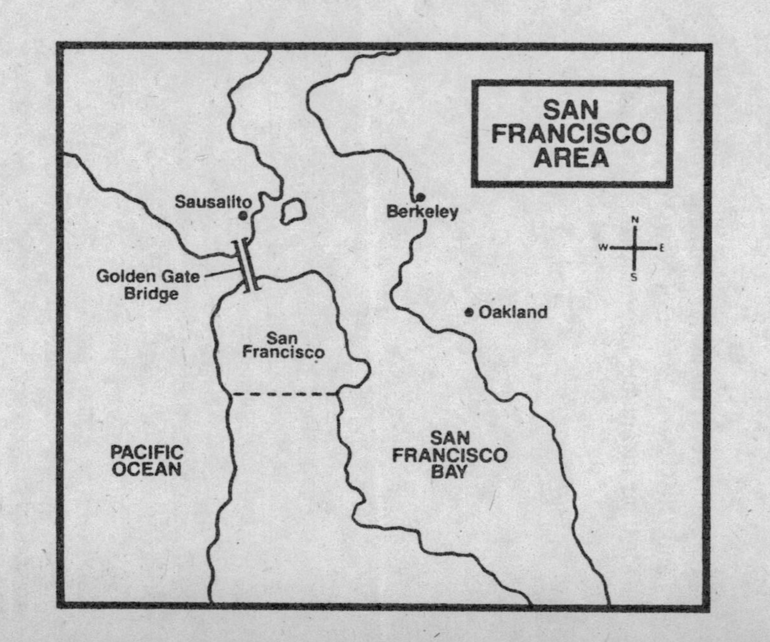
SAN FRANCISCO AREA
N
W
E
S
Sausalito
Berkeley
Oakland
Golden Gate Bridge
San Francisco
PACIFIC OCEAN
SAN FRANCISCO BAY

Chapter One

The view outside the bus window was simply magical. Kay Devore sighed and stared out at the mountains that cast giant shadows as the orange-red sun began to set. They were in Utah now—she'd seen a sign about three miles back. After Utah came Nevada, and then California. By two o'clock that morning they'd be in San Francisco. Kay would be home again.

She shifted uncomfortably in her seat and smoothed her wavy ash-blond hair out of her face. Home? Was it home anymore? Would it ever be home again? Well, she told herself firmly, plastering a set smile on her delicate face, she was going to make it her home. She was going to begin life all over again.

"Where are we?" The plump brunette beside her stretched and yawned.

"Utah," Kay told her quietly, fixing her cat-green eyes on the magnificent scenery.

"Boy, this is a long ride," the girl complained. "My name's Lisa, by the way. Lisa Parkins."

"Hi, I'm Kay Devore." The two women shifted in their cramped seats so they could shake hands. "And I got on in Golden, Colorado, so I know what you mean by long!" She laughed, the low musical laugh that Alan had always said sounded like the gentle roaring inside a seashell.

"Colorado! Why didn't you fly?" Lisa asked frankly, taking in Kay's good linen slacks and fawn-colored suede jacket—indications that she could have afforded a plane ticket. "If I didn't need every single penny for my tuition this year, I sure would've taken a plane. I'm a junior at Stanford," Lisa went on chattily. "What's the matter? You afraid of flying or something?"

She was so open and totally honest that Kay had to give her a straight answer. "Well," she began, "I thought about flying. But I decided I needed time to think, and lots of it. I've . . . um, been away from home for a while and I've been working a lot of stuff out in my head. I figured a long trip back would be good for me."

"Hey," Lisa breathed. "I really know where you're coming from. I had all these problems with my boyfriend last semester, and when I finished my last exam—I'm a biology major—I said to him, 'Eddie, you've got to let me breathe. I'm going to spend Christmas with my mother.' And I did, even though he ranted and raved."

"I spent Christmas with my mother, too," Kay confessed. "She has an apartment in Golden."

"You having man trouble too?" Lisa asked sympathetically.

Kay paused and stared down at her long tapered fingers, at the diamond sparkling beside the gold band on her left hand. "Yes, I guess you could call it that."

"Oh!" Lisa gulped, following Kay's gaze. "You're married!"

"I sure am." Kay leaned back in her seat and let the feelings wash over her. There was so much in her head that the pain felt crowded out. She was married, but she hadn't seen Alan in three months. She was a competent career woman, a marine biologist, and yet she felt like this schoolgirl, all young and vulnerable. She felt younger than her sister, Erica, younger than Alan, and yet older than the universe. It was going to be hard to forget her pain and grief, but she was determined to do just that.

"You left him?" Lisa ventured. "I don't mean to pry." Her round face was flushed and curious.

"We'd had problems; something happened," Kay muttered, more to herself than to Lisa. "But life goes on, doesn't it? And you can't sit around feeling sorry for yourself forever. At least, I can't."

It was just this determination, this total independence of spirit, that had pushed Kay over every other hurdle in her life. Getting her Ph.D. at Berkeley; helping her mother, Katherine, move out of the big house on Elkin Street when her father died; struggling with Alan through the first years when they barely had an extra few dollars for a movie or a night on the town. And then there was that last hurdle, the one she couldn't clear, the one that had made her stumble and reach out blindly for something, anything, to take away the searing pain that threatened to split her in two. She was only thirty-three but after the tragedy she felt a hundred. And so she'd run away, hoping to find comfort and solace and some remnants of a happy past.

That was why she'd gone to Colorado, to recapture the shifting colors and pure massiveness of the Rockies. How could anyone stand before the awesome sight of those mountains and that gigantic sky above them and feel sorry for herself? When she was little she used to sit nested into the oak window seat of her folks' big house on Elkin Street, watching the sun set behind those mountains, dreaming her dreams.

Wasn't it odd? she thought suddenly. She loved the mountains, but she'd fled to the sea to become a marine biologist. It was strange how opposites attracted her. She seemed to have some kind of unconscious but deliberate impulse within her to embrace the opposite of what she had, of what was familiar. And it was the same with men, she realized suddenly, sitting up straighter. She'd left Alan in Sausalito and found Johnny in Golden, two people so fundamentally different that it surprised Kay that she could have ever been close to both of them. Of course, what she felt for Johnny was simple friendship. It had nothing at all in common with her feelings for Alan. And yet there was a kind of easygoing quality to Johnny that had appealed to her, and made her come at least partway out of her shell.

Just like some old crustacean, she thought, smiling. Like a periwinkle, sticking out its head to see what was around and then quickly retreating back inside. Because going home to her mother and finding Johnny had basically been a stopgap, a little time out for breathing.

She had returned to the scene of the old happy times and found that they, too, were only memories, part of the past. It didn't help that her mother urged her every single day to go back to Alan and face up to reality.

"Besides," Katherine had insisted as they sat over coffee in her attractive one-bedroom apartment, "you have responsibilities, Kay. Do you think that job will sit there and wait for you forever?"

"Maybe," Kay had said, not sure herself. "They seem to like my work."

"The California Academy of Sciences can throw out a net any old day and haul in a new marine biologist who's an expert in sea urchins. Don't you read the papers? All those academic types out of work?"

"Mom . . ." Kay had cautioned.

"That is the absolute truth. Not that I care about your old sea urchins," Katherine had gone on, shaking a finger in her daughter's face. "I care about your husband. He's lonely, you're lonely, and you two have to work things out. Together."

Kay felt a tug at her arm. "Gee, you look awfully upset about something," Lisa told her frankly. "I hope I didn't get you all worked up."

"Oh!" Kay laughed in embarrassment. "Did I fade out on you? Sorry." She wasn't really, but her politeness quotient was way down these days. With

Johnny, and even with her mother, she hadn't had to be polite. And they were about the only people she'd talked to for three months.

They talked for a while longer, with Lisa explaining her plans for the future. Then she said, "I'm going to catch a few more winks before we get to the end of the line. Don't mean to be rude, but I'm just beat. And once I get back to school, Eddie's not going to give me much rest." She giggled, then huddled deeper into her bulky knit sweater. Resting her head on the back of the vinyl seat, she closed her eyes and quickly fell asleep.

Kay looked at the girl with something like wistfulness in her green, perceptive eyes. In a way Lisa reminded Kay of how she herself had been about fifteen years earlier. A bright, hopeful biology major, she'd said, ready to jump into the arms of the man she loved and discover a cure for cancer at the same time. It had been hard to listen to Lisa talk about her life plans without smiling a little—she had such a neat and uncomplicated view of things, a perfect schedule of events for a fulfilling and rewarding life. After she graduated from Stanford she planned to go to veterinary school, then start up her own practice near Red Bluff in the Sacramento Valley. Eddie would be a doctor, an ophthalmologist. They would have a couple of kids. She had the whole thing on a timer, all mapped out, without any provisions for life's great hitches and disappointments. Lisa had no contingency plans for failure—or worse.

Kay's finely etched features clouded as she gazed at the sleeping girl. Should I tell her? she wondered. But no, that would be a lousy thing to do to someone so happy and hopeful, someone who didn't have a clue as to what could happen in a life.

A life like Kay's. Well, she had to admit, before the horror of the tragedy, things had really gone well for her. She loved her work and was considered one of the top people in the business. She adored her little house in Sausalito with its lovely view of the bay and the boats lined up at the dock like so many tin soldiers, their masts clanking in the stiff breeze. She was nuts about her crazy sister, Erica, who maintained that, one day, the right agent or producer or director would see her and sign her up for a major motion picture. Until that day she'd take what acting parts she could get and do temp work to pay the rent.

And more than anything, Kay loved her husband. Alan Devore had been her best friend, her lover, her alter ego. He never failed to send shivers through her slender, petite form whenever he touched so much as a finger of her hand. She loved to look at him, at his broad shoulders—usually encased in a herringbone jacket with elbow patches—and long legs, at his sad, soulful eyes the color of brown velvet, at his full lips set into a stern, serious line.

But his was also a mouth that could laugh, filled with joy and teasing. And a mouth that could kiss tenderly, passionately, driving Kay wild with desire. Then there was his curly dark hair, shorn close to his head for practicality, and his trim beard—dark on his cheeks, reddish on his chin, brindled with silver throughout. She would run her hands through that beard and hair while he held her and caressed her arms, her back, her breasts. Then she would run her lips across his mouth and erase the deeply etched lines that had once been just a little boy's dimples. Her lips would complete the circle, up past his ear to the small scar over his left eye that he had gotten during basic training in the Navy. How he hated the fact that it wasn't really an old war wound, he had confessed once, because he thought she would find that more romantic.

"*More* romantic!" she'd gasped as he eased her clothing off and placed her gently on their large bed beneath the bay windows. "How could you possibly get any more romantic than you already are?"

"I'm going to keep trying," he warned her suggestively. And then, without words, he had shown her that, even in a marriage of eight years' standing, there were things about their bodies that had not yet been explored.

Kay's stomach tightened as she remembered their ecstatic lovemaking. Alan had been like a fire inside her that glowed cheerily on winter nights and sparked into a bonfire on sultry summer evenings. Even now she could feel him moving over her. It had been three long months since she'd seen him, and the loss of him was palpable.

Everyone had always said that they had the perfect marriage. The two of them would blanch when they heard that, as if a jinx were being put over them. Not that it wasn't true, but you were never supposed to say things like that out loud for fear you'd be testing the fates and that one of them, in its whimsical way, would slap you down hard.

Kay turned back to the window, to the brilliant constellations, like diamonds scattered over a black field. Alan had always been, for her, a brilliant magical gem, the center of her life. She missed him like crazy, and it drove her wild to think of the long months when she hadn't enjoyed the warmth of his touch.

Of course she'd see him—that was inevitable. They both worked at the California Academy of Sciences, she at the Steinhardt Aquarium and he at the Morrison Planetarium, where he was a radio astronomer. She recalled perfectly the day he'd received his acceptance in the mail. A week later hers had arrived.

"Perfect!" he'd exclaimed. "We don't have to buy a second car." He had swept the hair off the back of her neck and planted a resounding kiss on the nape.

"Nice," she'd remarked. "I get a plum position at Steinhardt and all you can think about is saving gas!"

"No," he'd responded, nuzzling her until she could scarcely stand straight. "I was actually thinking of all those cozy lunches we could have in my office. I've put in a requisition for a couch, you know. And I'm tucked away at the end of that long corridor with a nice thick door that can keep us inside and everybody else out."

"This is lunch you're talking about?" she'd asked with a laugh in her voice.

"Well . . ." He'd smiled lasciviously. "Not *only* lunch. Maybe sometimes we can skip the sandwiches altogether."

Kay forced the memories from her mind as the bus driver told them about an upcoming rest stop.

"Reno, Nevada, folks. Only ten minutes, now," he informed them over the loudspeaker. The big bus pulled into a roadside-diner parking lot and chugged to a halt. Kay looked over at her seatmate, but Lisa was still sleeping soundly.

"I'll bring you a coffee," Kay whispered as she climbed over the woman. She moved out with the thin stream of passengers into the darkness. It was chilly in the desert, nearly as cold as it had been in Colorado, and Kay pulled her jacket closed and zipped it as she hurried into the warmth of the diner. She let everyone else precede her to the takeout counter and made her way to the public phone in the back.

"Operator, this is a collect call from Kay Devore to San Francisco. The number is 415-555-9387."

There was a lot of clicking, then a dial tone, and finally a ringing on the other end.

"Hello?" she heard the operator say. "Collect call for anyone from Kay Devore."

"Collect!" Erica's voice was sharp and annoyed. "Are you kidding?"

"I'll pay you when I get there, sis, I promise." Kay laughed.

"Will you accept the charges, miss?" The operator was beginning to get a little testy.

"Well, what can I do? All right, I'll accept." Erica sighed. "But not willingly."

"Look," Kay said, nestling the phone more comfortably on her shoulder. "I'm doing this for your own good, so you won't have to go running around at all hours. The bus is a little late, so don't come meet me, all right? We're in Reno now—

that's about five hours away. We probably won't get in till two or so, and a struggling young actress needs her beauty sleep."

"Ooh, I'm so happy you're coming home," Erica bubbled excitedly. "Really, I'm beautiful enough as it is, and I never go to sleep till two anyway."

"No, I said." Kay smiled, imagining her funny, pretty sister, at twenty-eight the real beauty of the family. Erica was as tall as Kay was petite, with snapping blue eyes and a wild unruly mane of golden Shirley Temple curls. Naturally her looks usually relegated her to the roles of lightweight, goofy blondes—roles Erica had been trying to escape ever since she was a theater major at UCLA. She kept telling directors that she was worthy of more, and they kept telling her to take what she could get. Erica had never been really eager-beaver and aggressive about changing her theatrical image, but one day, she assured Kay, she would mature into her real persona and then she'd be turning down scripts right and left.

"Don't be a meanie," Erica teased. "I've got a hundred million things to catch up on with you, so I intend to stay up all night for girl talk. We could use a real heart-to-heart. By the way, how's Mom?"

"Great. She sends her love. Erica, this is *my* dime, remember, and my bus is going to pull out. Just stay where you are and I'll come in quietly. I've got the key."

"We'll see," Erica persisted.

"Go to bed, silly," Kay chided. "'Bye now." She replaced the receiver on its hook, and there was a smile on her face. She was nuts about her sister, and undoubtedly staying with her for a while until she got her bearings would be the best medicine in the world. Then she'd go apartment hunting, starting near the Academy of Sciences and working her way out from there. It had to be close enough by bus or subway so that commuting without a car wouldn't be a hassle.

Yes, Kay thought to herself as she went to the counter and ordered two coffees, I'll start over by myself. I've got plenty of resources, lots of inner strength and a will to survive, don't I? Otherwise I wouldn't have made it this far.

Kay glanced down the counter, where a young couple were sharing a sandwich and sipping coffee. The woman was holding a baby wrapped in a bright red bunting, rocking it gently over her shoulder. The baby was fast asleep, oblivious of the clatter of cups and plates and of its parents' conversation.

The mother noticed Kay staring at her child. "Dead to the world," she said to Kay with a friendly smile, glancing over at her sleeping infant.

Kay didn't respond. A numbing cold had gripped her insides and wouldn't let go.

She quickly paid the waitress and hugged the bag to her chest, stepping out into the parking lot. The hot coffee warmed her a little, but not enough. She'd been away from work too long, that was it, she told herself, and from Erica's sunny disposition. She needed to lose herself in her job and to carve out a new life, and then things would turn around. She just knew they would.

Lisa was still asleep, so Kay climbed back over

her and placed one coffee carefully on the floor beside the girl's bag. She opened the other and sniffed the steam, then gingerly took a sip. It burned her tongue, but it tasted marvelous. It reminded her of all those coffees she'd shared with Johnny in Golden for the last three months.

He had said that she seemed so sad he'd have to cheer her up. Naturally he had no idea why she was sad, but one of the things she liked about Johnny Pallas was that he never asked questions, never pried into her past. He was a man who lived purely for the present and had no pretensions whatsoever. Maybe, Kay had thought when she met him, maybe some of his lightheartedness will rub off on me.

She watched the highway slip past, the dark buildings and rock formations disappearing into the night. The first time she had met Johnny, she recalled, he had been sitting with her mother, sharing coffee and discussing plans for the bookcases he was going to build for her. When Kay walked into the room he had smiled, a friendly open grin, and pushed his long, dirty-blond hair out of his face. He was tan and boyish-looking with dark blue eyes set in an innocent face. His ears stuck out a little when he smoothed his hair back over them.

"Kay"—Katherine had nodded—"this is Johnny Pallas. I found him in the Yellow Pages."

"And am I ever glad you did, Mrs. Rogers," he had said with a hearty laugh. "Your mom and I have been trying to figure a way to make this modern box of a place look a little more homey," he told Kay.

"She misses the old house on Elkin Street so

much," Kay had commiserated, taking a seat while her mother went to get her a cup of coffee. "After a big old Victorian, this place is like a prison cell for her."

"I know just what you mean," Johnny had agreed, leaning back from the table. His long beanpole legs ended in big feet clad in a well-worn pair of leather boots. "I grew up in a house just like that in the Berkshires, in Massachusetts. Nothing like those old houses."

It was easy to talk to Johnny about anything and everything, from rafting down the Colorado to his favorite recipe for pumpkin pie. He wasn't awed by Kay's credentials and prestigious job as so many men were, nor did he feel that it was essential to discover everything about her in one week. He was a charmer, though. He stretched that bookcase job, which should have taken him a day, into ten days, although he only charged half of what his skilled craftsmanship should have demanded. Even the normally no-nonsense Katherine had been sad to see him finish and pack up his tools. Kay hadn't actually thought much about his leaving, so wrapped up had she been in her own somber thoughts. And when she met him again she felt comfortable, but not overjoyed. The only man she would have sold her soul to see was Alan, but that, of course, had been impossible.

She met Johnny again at the Eagle's Nest, a neighborhood pub near the room she'd rented in Golden. There were many nights when she simply couldn't face the empty walls of that room and the silences of her own heart, when she couldn't replay her shame and guilt once more or discuss her problems with her mother one more time.

On those nights she went over to the Eagle's Nest, just to be around people. It was never too crowded or noisy, there was no jukebox, and thankfully, no singles. She could spend an entire evening over a hamburger and a beer without getting hassled, and Ella, the pub's only waitress, would feed her an endless supply of paper place mats on which Kay scribbled and sketched hundreds of research ideas for her sea urchins. She was supposedly on a leave of absence from the lab, and she knew that she'd better have some great experiments planned for her return, or her supervisor, Dr. David Kalens, would have her head.

Toward the end of the evening, when most of the customers had straggled home, Ella would draw herself a beer, drag up a chair to Kay's table and watch whatever basketball or hockey game was on TV. She'd also talk Kay's ear off, criticizing the game, the players and especially the announcers. Kay would just listen or not, as she chose.

But one night a familiar face turned up at Kay's table. "Can I sit down?" its owner asked, turning a chair around and sitting on it backwards.

"Hi, Johnny." Kay smiled.

They spent a lot of time together after that. He was just so easy to be with, so unthreatening and full of fun. His attitude toward each new day was summed up in the proverb "If life hands you lemons, make lemonade." And, as he said that first night, "Anyone who looks so sad needs someone to squeeze those lemons for her."

"Well, tell me, how did you get to Colorado from the Berkshires, anyway?" she'd asked him, smiling at last.

"Let's see," he began, leaning his chair toward her and winking. "I dropped out of the University of Massachusetts in my junior year and hitchhiked to Denver to be a ski bum. Not that I knew anything about skiing, but it sounded like a great thing to do. I was going to conquer the ski jump, fly down the slopes, then retire to the lodge in the evenings and wait for the ski bunnies to melt all over me. But"—Johnny chuckled—"it didn't work out that way. See, my first time out I veered off the ramp, made quick friends with a couple of pines and broke my leg in three places. Thank the Lord I was listening when my grandpa tried to drum some carpentry skills into my head long ago. They've kept me from eating snow out here in Colorado. And I love the mountains, love the big sky, so I've stayed on. Now I'm twenty-seven, and I guess I've found my life work. Until something better comes along." He shrugged.

Kay smiled understandingly, intrigued and delighted with his ability and determination to make the most of a bad situation. If only she could be more like that. If only Alan could be . . .

She was honest with Johnny up to a point. She told him that she was married and having problems, that she'd gone away for a while to think things out. She never burdened him or their relationship with her personal tragedy. It was just so refreshing to spend time with someone who didn't know, who didn't offer blind sympathy or give her a look that implied that he was sure she was going to break into a zillion pieces at any moment. She didn't want to spoil anything with Johnny. He was as uncomplicated as two-plus-two, and she liked that, because she and Alan were as involved and intricate as the most difficult mathematical theorem ever devised.

Kay sighed and fished around in her purse for her lipstick. She looked at her watch in the dim overhead light. Midnight, exactly. Johnny was the complete opposite of Erica, who loved staying up all night. He always called their evenings short so he could get up with the dawn. Or sometimes, on weekends, when he wasn't working, he'd be waiting on her doorstep to take her on a picnic or to a movie. It was odd, but she never thought of those outings as dates. And she never once felt as though she was betraying Alan by spending time with another man. Johnny was a balm for her wounds, and she needed him.

Was she physically attracted to Johnny? That was hard to say. He was handsome, but so were dozens of men. Sex was out of the question for Kay, and strangely enough, they never even discussed it. He respected the distance she wanted to keep. As for her own feelings, it was simply too soon to think of being with another man. Or maybe it was too late. No one else's touch could ever fill the void left by not having Alan's, Kay was certain of that, and she didn't have to experiment to find out. She was hollow inside, and only he could fill that space.

The bus turned onto Route 40, and Kay realized that her destination was barely an hour away. What would she find there? she wondered. In a way it was good to be getting back, even though San

Francisco had been the place where the most terrible thing she could ever have dreamed in a nightmare had actually happened. Despite that, and despite her fears for the future, she had to return and pick up where she'd left off. She intended to throw herself into her work, spend a lot of time with Erica, read some good books and catch up with a few select old friends. And get back with Alan . . . if he'd take her back . . . if she could . . .

Eventually she'd be able to see Alan again, she knew. That was going to take more out of her than anything else, but she would steel herself against her own memories and, by God, she'd do it. She couldn't bear the thought of losing her husband—her best friend. As for divorce, that was completely and totally out of the question. Even if they only remained married on paper, they were still bound by something stronger than the pull of the tides, the turning of the earth or the blinding brilliance of a star.

Those stars. She looked up at the bright pattern of white dots flaked across the night sky, circling a hazy moon with a spray of clouds across it. She could never stare at that particular view without thinking of Alan, of course, because he was an astronomer by profession and a stargazer by nature. His moods were as changeable as the seasons—Kay had never known anyone to be as down when it rained and as happy when the skies were blue as Alan was. She'd never minded the moodiness, though. The intensity of his feelings and the honesty of his emotions were two of the things she loved most about him. He never, ever sidestepped an issue with her, and when he gave his love he gave it unceasingly, almost exhaustingly. And she knew that it was all hers.

We used to look at those stars together, she thought with a pang of remembrance. On clear nights Alan would set up his telescope on the back deck of their house in Sausalito and study the skies, like an ancient explorer searching for a new route or a small boy looking for a spaceship. Kay would sit quietly beside him and watch the night and the man she loved as the sounds of clanging masts and rigging wafted up to them from the docks below. Then, without speaking a word, they would reach out and their fingers would entwine. Sometimes they'd sit like that for hours.

God, how she loved him! The tears came unbidden to her eyes and she fought them back. She mustn't think like that. Even though she loved him more than she could bear, Kay feared that it could never be the same between them.

She brushed a stray tear away and Alan's image vanished with it. But only temporarily, of course. His face, his body, every part of his being, was imprinted on her soul. That was something she would simply have to live with, and maybe, after a long while, she would get used to it.

"San Francisco," the driver called out. "All passengers going on to points south please keep your seats."

Kay gathered her belongings and the girl beside her stirred and opened her eyes.

"What time is it?" Lisa yawned.

"Two A.M.," Kay told her. "Have a good rest of your trip, Lisa."

"Oh, wow," the girl breathed. "You're home."

"That I am." Kay smiled ruefully. "For better or worse." She bit her lip, gave Lisa a final good-bye and made her way down the aisle to the exit door.

Chapter Two

The driver lifted her two suitcases from the hold below the bus and Kay hoisted them, along with her tote, into the main depot. She hated bus terminals. There was something so lonely and comfortless about them.

There were a few derelicts stretched out on the wooden benches, and one big family all huddled in a group, the mother nodding over the infant in her lap. There was a marine, sitting erect next to his duffel bag, trying not to fall asleep, and a couple of sailors beside him, smoking quietly. An older woman in a tattered fur coat was making her way slowly around the station, mumbling aloud.

Kay licked her lips and walked on past the ticket booths, most of them shut up for the night. At least she was there, in her city, back at home base. She'd grab a cab and be at Erica's in no time.

I hope that nut didn't come to pick me up, she thought. She smiled to herself, thinking of her sister's insistence that she would be there to greet Kay.

She saw the sign ahead of her, "To Buses and Taxis," and started toward it, struggling under the weight of her luggage. Naturally the bags held more books than clothes—that was how she always packed. "No one," her mother had joked when she saw Kay open those suitcases, "could ever accuse you of traveling light! When do you find time to read all those books?"

"I inhale them in my sleep, Mother," Kay had responded.

She grunted and kept walking, past the vending machines and on toward another, smaller waiting room that led to the exit.

Then suddenly she stopped dead in her tracks with a gasp. "Oh, no!" The words escaped her lips even as she tried to suppress them. It was Alan, sitting on a bench, intent on the book in his hands. Kay started and blinked, then looked at him through glazed eyes as a storm of emotions whipped through her.

How had he known she'd be arriving that night? Why had he come? She simply wasn't ready to face him. Not now. Not yet. A surge of panic made her want to turn and run into the dark night, but she couldn't tear her eyes from his face. Her heart was pounding around in her chest like a caged bird and it would have been impossible to say whether it was due to the fear of confronting him or the fact that she loved him so purely, so intensely. Her gaze remained steady even when her eyes filled with tears.

She had forgotten how fiercely handsome he was, how every part of him combined to make one perfect entity. His body was a trim, long muscular column. His dark curly hair and his beard were starting to show a bit more gray, she noticed—had they changed only in recent months?—but it was becoming on him; it suited his mature attractiveness. His trench coat hung open, revealing a black turtleneck and jeans, and she could see that there were deep circles under his eyes.

Then, as if he could feel her presence, Alan suddenly looked up from his book, his penetrating dark eyes under their thick brows boring into Kay. The pain and the hurt and the passion that had been pent up inside him for so long were reflected in the angular planes of his craggy face. He didn't have to say a word for her to read his intention. His eyes haunted her, as they had all the time they'd been apart. They penetrated her very being and spoke directly to her, telling her that she hadn't been out of his thoughts since she'd left him three months earlier.

Slowly he got to his feet, his eyes never releasing hers. "Kay," he whispered hoarsely. "Kay!" he called to her.

She shut her eyes and two tears clung doggedly to her long lashes. "No," she moaned despite her desire to hold him again.

"We have to talk." His tone was demanding. It told her that she couldn't escape him, no matter how hard she tried.

"There's nothing to talk about," she choked out.

"Kay, for God's sake! Don't play games with me." He got up and walked toward her, and she found that she couldn't move away. The suitcases turned to lead in her hands, but she was unable to put them down. Alan did it for her, gently prying the handles from her fingers. The warmth of his hands was too much, too soon. She gasped and whipped away from him, leaving him to drop her bags on the floor.

"Three months is a very long time when all you can do is think about a person who isn't there, Kay. I want my wife back," he breathed heavily. "More than anything else in the world."

She couldn't be coy with him, not after everything they'd been through together. All she could do was meet his strength with her own. Before, right after it happened, she hadn't been able to fight back. It felt good, in an odd way, to let the feelings out now. "Don't push me, Alan," she warned. "I'll let you know when I'm coming back."

"That's great. What are you going to do? Send me a telegram? 'Finally over it, able to live again'? Just fine, Kay," he snarled. "And what do you intend to do in the meantime? What am *I* supposed to do?" He reached out and grabbed her wrist, pulling her closer. "No, that's not good enough for me. I've waited long enough."

She was completely put off by his tone and the way he was ordering her around, demanding that she do exactly as *he* said.

"And do you think it's been easy for me?" she exclaimed. "Going away was crucial. It was something I had to do for myself—and for us. But that doesn't mean the time just sped by on wings of song. Give me a little credit, would you?"

"When are you going to come to your senses?" he suddenly yelled, his handsome face coloring with rage. Several people passing through the waiting room turned to stare at the couple who were facing off like a couple of angry bears. "Life goes on, Kay, and you can't hide from it. All you can do is take the hand that reaches out and grab onto it like a lifeline. Well?" he demanded.

"Not yet!" she yelled, shocked at herself. To defy this man and his love was criminal, but she simply had to do it. Without even thinking about it, she fled toward the exit sign, hoping there would be a taxi parked right at the doorway. She didn't dare to look back, knowing he was pursuing her.

After shouldering her way through the glass doors of the bus station, she stepped out into the street, her eyes wild and frantic. All she knew was that she had to get away from him now. Some other time she'd be able to gaze into those caring angry eyes, but not tonight.

Through her tears she saw a familiar sight and sobbed with relief. It was Erica's unmistakable orange VW Beetle with the missing front fender, parked on the opposite side of the street. As Kay struggled toward it she could see the mass of blond hair strewn over the back of the driver's seat. She ran to the car as well as she could with her luggage, never daring to glance over her shoulder at the man who stood looking at her through the glass doors.

"Erica!" Kay choked out. "Erica, wake up!" The window was nearly rolled up to the top, so she shouted again. "Erica, for heaven's sake!"

"Hmmm." Her sister's wide blue eyes fluttered open. "Sis!" She smiled and stretched, pulling herself up in the seat like a sleepy cat. "Nice to see you."

"Erica, will you unlock this door! C'mon, quick." She grabbed the handle as Erica flipped the button upward, but she couldn't stop herself from looking up as she did so. There was Alan, standing in the harsh light just outside the station. He didn't run to her or call her. He simply fixed that stern, intense gaze of his on her and she shriveled inside, realizing how much he cared. She forced her way into the tiny car, dumping her bags over the seat into the back.

"Let's get out of here," she muttered to Erica.

"Whatsa matter, sis? Some guy put the moves on you in the depot?" Erica asked, turning the key in the ignition. "Look, it happens to me all the time. You just have to ignore them and eventually they go away. If they don't, you can give 'em a good swift kick!"

"That's not what's wrong," Kay practically yelled. "Would you please start this car?" She was desperate to get away, out of his accusing sight.

Erica revved the engine and tore off down the street, running a yellow light. "I don't think long bus rides are good for you," she told Kay, keeping her foot down on the gas pedal. "You're acting weird, paranoid. Like somebody's chasing you."

Kay rubbed her face and ran her hands through her tousled hair. "He didn't chase me . . . I ran away . . . again. Dammit."

"Who? What are you talking about?"

"Alan," Kay exploded. "He was there."

"Alan!" Erica repeated, instantly slowing down. "For God's sake, Kay, why should you run away from your own husband?"

"I wish I knew," Kay whispered so softly that she seemed to be talking to herself, not her sister, who stopped for a red light, then turned with a sigh to stare at Kay. "What is it?" Kay asked. "What do you see, Erica?"

"I'm not sure," her sister murmured, her lovely face creased with concern. "But whatever it is there behind your eyes, it doesn't look so hot to me."

"I'm afraid you're very perceptive," Kay told her. "This hasn't been the greatest three months, you know. And here I was, all set to start my life again, do everything right. Then *he* had to show up so suddenly. I just wasn't ready . . . not yet."

"Why don't you tell me about it?" Erica asked softly as she drove toward her Union Street apartment.

Erica clicked on the lights and hastily swept aside the newspapers lying on the couch. "Home sweet home," she proclaimed, ushered Kay inside the cluttered one-bedroom apartment. "Smaller than a postage stamp, but all mine, you know. Well, take off your jacket and stay awhile." She moved Kay's suitcases to one side of the living-room-cum-kitchen while Kay removed her suede jacket and hung it on the bentwood stand by the door. Her high-necked beige georgette blouse was wrinkled from hours of traveling, but the usually fastidious Kay didn't seem to notice.

"What I cannot figure out," Kay murmured,

moving some unironed laundry off the overstuffed chair so that she could sit down, "is how Alan knew I was coming in tonight by bus."

"Don't look at me," Erica yelped, throwing off her multicolored poncho. "I swear to you, sis, I didn't tell. Actually, I haven't talked to Alan in a month."

Kay gave her a quizzical look. "A month, huh? What did you talk about before then?"

"Kay . . ." Erica sat across from her on the couch and helped herself to a handful of nuts and raisins from the bowl on the rustic oak-slab coffee table. "I happen to like Alan. I was worried about him. He was awfully lonely. And he wanted to know if I'd heard from you."

"What did you say?" Kay hated questioning her sister like this, but having actually seen Alan in the station had brought his presence back to her so forcibly that she felt compelled to ask about him, like a starving person attacking her first meal.

"I said you were about as lousy as he was. No lie, right, sis?" Erica smiled.

"But I hadn't decided to come back a month ago," Kay persisted, getting up and going to the window. "So how did he know?"

"Must have been Mom," Erica surmised. "Every time I've talked to her lately she's gotten on my case about Alan. You'd think she was *his* mother, the way she talks about him."

"Don't I know it," Kay muttered. Katherine had been nagging her about going back to Alan ever since she had arrived in Golden.

"But I think he's pretty wonderful myself," Erica went on, putting her feet up on the coffee table. "Handsome, brilliant, caring, well-adjusted—"

"Not all *that* well-adjusted," Kay protested. How could she make her sister understand that a great barrier, a deep chasm, had opened up between her and her husband?

"Well, what do you expect, for heaven's sake!" Erica's usually devil-may-care whimsy vanished and her blue eyes suddenly took on an annoyed cast. "You think you were the only one with a tragedy? It happened to him, too, you know." She was nearly yelling and looked anxiously at the far wall. An elderly invalid lived on the other side and she hated noise, particularly at two-thirty in the morning.

"I know." Kay nodded.

"Sorry, sis. I just got carried away." Erica shrugged off the somber moment and grinned, back to normal. "Want some coffee?"

"No, thanks. I'd never get to sleep." Actually, Kay didn't see how she would close her eyes at all that night, with or without caffeine. It was just that she hadn't been prepared, hadn't expected to see Alan; that was why she'd gotten so bollixed up about him. All her resolve to mend slowly and put herself into the right frame of mind before seeing him again was completely gone. It had vanished in that moment in the bus station when he'd called her name with such love, such fierce passion.

"Well, I need something. Let's have a beer," Erica suggested, going to the little pink half-refrigerator that stood forlornly in the middle of her kitchen area. Erica had painted it herself one afternoon in desperation, and when Kay asked about the shocking pink, Erica's response had been, "Bright colors make things look larger. And since I can't afford a full-size one, I decided to make this one look as big as possible."

"I guess I wouldn't object to that." Kay sighed. She eased off her boots, revealing small, delicate feet which she massaged one after the other. "Don't you have to work tomorrow?" she asked.

"Nope. I took the day off 'cause you were coming home. That's why I love temp work. The pay's lousy, but you can make your own hours. Leaves me free for auditions and such." She popped the tops off two beers and poured them into tall glasses. "And what money I do bring home goes for pictures and résumés, yogurt, wheat germ and beer." She brought the glasses over and plopped herself down on the couch.

"How's the career coming?" Kay asked softly.

Her sister's brow furrowed. "Pretty terrible. I don't know why I keep it up, actually, except I suppose I'm addicted. Do you remember how certain I was when I got out of UCLA, not just about my first Oscar, but my second and third? Ha!" She gave a scornful laugh.

"Well, you did get all the leads in college," Kay pointed out.

"And how far is college from real life? About as far as the earth from that star Alan's always beaming things off of. What's it called?"

"Andromeda," Kay murmured. There was Alan again, smack in the middle of their conversation.

"Yeah. About seventeen hundred light-years, by my calculation. I remember that summer I got out of school, you and Mom and Dad had to hold me back by the hair to keep me from racing to New York so I could scout out all the plays on Broadway."

Kay took a sip of her beer and smiled at her sister. "You were going to discover which ones would be optioned for movies so you could pick the roles that would be best for you."

"What a dope I was! That was the summer you and Alan got your Ph.D.'s, you eager beavers."

"Erica." Kay leaned forward and touched her sister's hand. "Am I imagining it, or are you purposely bringing the topic back to Alan every time I change it?"

Erica gave her a sheepish grin. "I'm that obvious, huh?"

"You're perfectly blatant."

"Well, I thought you wanted to talk. You should have seen your face when we drove away from the bus depot. You looked like you'd seen a whole army of ghosts."

Suddenly Kay was crying again, for no reason she could think of. She didn't even bother to brush away the tears that coursed down her cheeks, so Erica reached over and did it for her. Then she hugged her big sister tightly.

"You'll never get Alan out of your system, Kay. Why don't you just go back to him right away? I'm sure if you give it half a chance you can work things out. You and Alan were the happiest couple I ever knew—even happier than Mom and Dad when he was alive. It would kill me to see that go down the tubes. Not to mention what it would do to you."

Kay sniffled back a few tears and shook her head. "It's not that simple, don't you see? We were great together when life was rosy, but afterward . . . you know, we were constantly picking on each other, blaming each other for everything. I started hating myself for what I was doing, but I couldn't stop. I guess he couldn't, either—it's like he was furious all the time."

"Wow, that's hard to believe. Alan's always been such a sweetie," Erica murmured. "Are you reading things into this? You know, Kay, I always thought your running off to Golden was a little precipitate."

Kay squeezed her eyes shut, holding back the flood of memories that threatened to overwhelm her. But it was too powerful, so she allowed it in. "He drove me away. We had a scene in my office just a week before I split."

Erica pursed her lips. "Listen, he may have been upset and overwrought, but he'd never drive you away. That man wanted you more than Romeo ever wanted Juliet. If you couldn't see that, you were blind. And he still does." She pounded her fist on the coffee table for emphasis.

"It's late . . ." Kay sighed, getting up. "I'll sleep on the couch, but I think I should get myself a place tomorrow. Somewhere near work. At least for a little while."

"Kay, you sit down and tell me all about that scene in your office. Stop avoiding issues."

Kay looked into her sister's face and saw how troubled she was, how much she meant every word. Clearly she was only trying to help. "All right." She settled herself back into the big chair.

"This was, let's see, about the middle of September. I'd really been in a bad state for weeks, moping around, aloof, despondent. He couldn't ignore that, of course, because Alan could never stand any breach between us. He always wanted to air things out, bring them out in the open."

"I remember," Erica commented.

"Well, he arranged for us to spend a weekend at our favorite getaway."

"The Homestead Inn?" Erica interrupted. "That gorgeous place on the Pacific Coast Highway, right near Big Sur?"

"You got it." Kay nodded. "He really wanted to go back to Mexico, to the place we went for our honeymoon, but I vetoed that idea immediately. I never could have stood being back where it all began between us."

"The Homestead sounds nothing like a compromise to me." Erica laughed. "So why didn't you go?"

"The Friday afternoon we were scheduled to leave, I was in the lab running a new test on my sea urchins."

"Skip the dull stuff," Erica urged her.

"It's not dull to me!" Kay barked. "Anyway, I was putting the information into the computer and it suddenly hit me that I wouldn't be able to stand being in a place where we were so happy together in the past. It would have seemed a mockery of our marriage to try to recapture that . . . that other couple, the one who existed before the tragedy."

"I disagree. You were still the same people. You still are now. With a hell of a lot to give each other."

"Just hear me out," Kay pleaded. She realized as she spoke that the lab was her haven. Even now, coming back from Golden, she was itching to get in there with her tanks and test tubes and computer printouts. She and her assistant, Ada Ortiz, had often worked late together after the tragedy, throwing themselves into their research with the kind of enthusiasm usually reserved for passionate love affairs. But the routine testing and recording of data had seemed to Kay to be the only real thing in her life at that point. It was the only thing she wanted to do.

"I called Alan over at the planetarium and said I wasn't going. It was just before six, I remember. I told him to go on without me."

Erica hooted with laughter. "My dear sister, one does not go to the Homestead Inn alone to stare at the trees and sit in the hot tub. The most romantic inn on the continent of America, and you tell him to go by himself! You're nuttier than I gave you credit for."

"I guess." Kay sighed. She took a long drink of her beer and put it down on the coffee table. "But I just couldn't go. I couldn't." She whispered the words with quiet desperation.

"So then what happened?" Erica prompted. "Alan's not the kind of person to leave it at, 'No, thanks, I don't think I want a marvelous romantic weekend with you right now.'"

"He certainly isn't. Or wasn't. It only took him five minutes to get from his office over to mine. I think he scared Ada out of her wits when he came storming into the lab and yelled at her to get out."

Erica giggled at the image of Kay's statuesque assistant, who wasn't scared of anything, running away from Alan.

"It's not funny, sis." Kay sighed. She sat back and thought about her husband and that day, and a shiver went through her.

It had been a warm sunny September afternoon, and golden light had suffused the lab with a warm beauty. The sterile equipment of science, the machines and heat lamps and tanks, seemed to have spotlights on them that day. After her quick conversation with Alan on the phone, Kay had gone right back to work, blocking out everything except the routine chores she had to perform.

"Look at this bunch, Ada," she called to her assistant. "See how they work their jaws?"

Ada Ortiz dipped the long-handled net into the large, well-lit tank and took one specimen out for examination. "What do you think would happen if we . . . ?"

They were interrupted by the sound of the double swinging doors crashing open. Alan burst through them, his strong jaw set and his face a mask of rage. He was a tall man, but he seemed gigantic when framed in the doorway.

"Ada, would you mind leaving us alone?" he growled without so much as looking at the woman. His eyes were fixed on Kay. "My wife and I have something to discuss."

"Of course, Dr. Devore," Ada murmured, already on her way out.

"Alan, I—" Kay raised a hand in feeble protest.

"Now, you listen to me." He stalked across the room to her, and she cringed, not in fear of his anger but in terror at what had ripped them apart. Every time she looked at him, she was reminded of it. "I've had it, Kay. You're taking me for granted and, what's worse, you're taking *us* for granted."

"Look," she mumbled, sinking into a chair. "I don't think you understand. I can't go off on this weekend. I really have a lot of work to do. My conference is Tuesday and I need every bit of data I can scrounge up by then."

He bent and took her by the shoulders, lifting her bodily from her seat. She could feel the strength in his large hands, hands that used to caress her and drive her into a frenzy of ecstasy. But no more. Although they'd continued to sleep in the same room, and even to make love, their passion had been silent and painful.

"You haven't heard a word I've said, Kay," he told her sternly. "And the thing is, you don't understand me. I need you. We have to work this thing out—you can't just retreat into your little shell and avoid it. That's why we have to get away, spend some time learning how to heal each other's wounds."

Kay's mind was a blank. She was numb to pain now, and to her husband's insistent demands. All she knew was that she had work to do. Or, rather, that was all she wanted to know. "I'm not going, Alan. It's as simple as that."

"Simple!" The word flew out of him like a bullet winging toward a target. "You care more about your damn barnacles than you do about me! What the hell is wrong with you, woman?"

Kay could only watch his rage, as though she were witnessing it from a great distance. She couldn't muster up the feelings to respond, so she just stood there and took it.

"Come on!" he yelled. "You love this book more than me, right?" He took her recently published text on marine biology and swept it off her desk onto the floor. "You're the consummate scientist, just a big, walking brain. No heart!" He hurled her notebooks to the floor, narrowly missing the big tank of sea urchins. "Come on! Fight back! Tell me you don't love me anymore. I want to hear you say it!" His deep brown eyes were burning coals, glowering at her, challenging her, and the cords of his neck stood out as he screamed, "By God, Kay, you have to let me in! You have to let us share this thing." He gave her desk a powerful shove and lunged for her, gripping her in a crushing embrace. He brought his mouth down on hers and she went limp in his arms.

Somewhere, way back behind her dark despair, she wanted to respond, to let herself be wooed and won, to forget the fear and anguish of the past months, but that was clearly impossible. Somewhere, back in that emotional vault she had locked so tightly, she was frightened, not only by her own reaction—or lack of it—but also by her husband's rage. She had never seen him this livid, never known that he had the capacity for such rage and violence. She stared down at the books he had scattered all over, and she felt . . . nothing. Not so much as a glimmer of shock.

"I thought I knew him as well as I did myself, Erica," Kay went on. "But I saw right then that I knew nothing at all about myself. I had no idea what made either of us tick; it was as if we were complete strangers. No, that's not even it. It was like . . ." She groped for an explanation. "Like we had just started out as human beings. We'd just been given all our body parts and organs, our brains and nerve endings and hearts, and we had to figure out all by ourselves what to do with them."

Erica shook her head in amazement. "That's pretty heavy. But I don't know, he was probably just trying to poke you a little, get you to open up. He was the same Alan."

"But I wasn't the same Kay. And I'm still not." She shook her head deliberately from side to side. "I can't tell you, just as I couldn't tell him that day what was different about me. I just knew I had to be away from him. That sounds crazy, doesn't it? Given the kind of relationship we had—have," she corrected herself. "But I couldn't help thinking that I'd never had any time alone to deal with it. I owed myself that."

"So you panicked and ran."

"It wasn't running," Kay cut in sharply. "Not the way you mean it."

"You think you would've stuck around if he hadn't gone ape and destroyed your lab?"

Kay reached over and gave her sister a playful push. "Let's not overdramatize this thing. He didn't destroy it. He just threw some books around."

"Kay! You're doing it again. Don't avoid the issue," Erica snapped. "You just said you were terrified because you'd never seen him so angry. So inside, to you, he might as well have wrecked the place."

"Oh," Kay breathed. "I see what you mean."

She bit her lip, then rested her head in her hands. "I have to get some sleep, sis. I'm so bleary."

"Okay. Me too. Sure you don't want another beer to put you out?" Erica offered.

"Uh-uh. Just a towel and a blanket." She got up and went wearily to her suitcase for her nightgown and toilet articles.

"Sleep late tomorrow morning," Erica advised her. "We'll talk some more when you feel like it."

"You're a nice sister." Kay smiled. She tossed the nightgown over one shoulder and walked across the room to Erica. The two women threw their arms around each other and hugged. They stood like that for a long moment.

"Sis," Erica said at last, moving back to look into Kay's face. "Tell the truth. Do you still love Alan?"

Kay stared at the floor for a second; then her bright green eyes met her sister's gaze. "More than anything," she affirmed.

"Then you haven't got a problem with him, because he loves you, too."

"Does he? Even now? I wonder," Kay murmured sadly.

"It's my firm opinion that the only problem you've got is *you*. And you better work on that one." Erica pummeled Kay lightly on the back.

"I guess you're right." Kay nodded. "It's just that there's so much going on inside me. I don't know what to do first."

Erica smiled, then squeezed Kay's hand. "You're a bright girl. Brilliant, in fact. I.Q. of at least one-forty-five. You'll figure it out."

"But that's my whole problem. I think too much."

"I mean you'll figure it out with your heart. If you let yourself. Go to bed, will you?"

Erica started for the tiny bathroom off the living room while Kay began to undress. She unzipped her slacks and eased them off her slender legs, then removed her blouse and bra. She burrowed into the sheer cotton nightgown like a bird into a warm nest and stretched herself out full length on the couch to wait for Erica to finish in the bathroom.

"Well, Kay," she whispered to herself. "You're home. Now you have to get started."

Chapter Three

"Good to have you back, Kay." Dr. David Kalens, a tiny gnome of a man who practically lived in his white lab coat, reached up to put an arm around Kay's shoulder.

"Thanks, David. I'm glad to be here again." They walked out of the long conference room and down the corridor to the elevator.

"Did I tell you that Pete at Woods Hole wants the stats on your urchins for his embryology work? I told him that if he publishes anything, if so much as a comic book hits the stands with your stuff not credited in it, I'll have his head. And he's up for tenure, so I don't think he'll play around."

"He's pretty tricky, though." Kay laughed. "When he was working in my lab I used to come in early just to catch him spooning out roe from my best specimens. Fish eggs are a delicacy, you know."

"And so are you." Dr. Kalens winked. "Tell Ada I'll have my secretary type up all the info and mail it to Pete whenever she assembles it."

"Will do." Kay watched him trundle down the corridor and smiled fondly after him. He was her mentor and had supervised all the work she'd done after her Ph.D. Unlike so many academics, he always gave credit where it was due, and no matter where he lectured, whether in California or Massachusetts or England or China, he invariably praised Dr. Kay Devore's work during his talks.

"Kay, I'm leaving now. My son's dentist appointment. Remember? I told you." Ada rushed around gathering her purse and jacket.

"You are?" Kay was slightly disappointed, but more in herself than in Ada. She hadn't remembered. "Oh, sure, see you tomorrow. Dr. Kalens wants some stuff pronto, but I'll put most of it together if you'll finish it up in the morning."

"Naturally. 'Bye, Kay."

Kay stood in the empty lab for a second, blinking in the fluorescent light. It felt so secure being there. She turned her attention to the row of glass tanks and picked up her clipboard to jot down the temperature readings.

Her first day back had reminded her that this was what she really missed—the staff conferences, the countless details of her research, a new shipment of urchins, the grant proposal she was writing with Ada and Dr. Vindalu in the next lab. She felt connected again in just these first few hours, as though she were competent and able to take care of things. People relied on her and looked up to her for professional advice, and that felt marvelous.

It was so different from the way she'd felt three months earlier with Alan. Then she hadn't been able to do anything right—things just fell apart in her hands. She'd hated all the fighting and worrying, the silent dinners and the empty evenings they'd shared. They had been exhausting in a way that her work never was. She vowed that as of that day she was only going to concentrate on her job. Later she could ease back into everything else.

The quiet burble of the air pumps soothed her, and she stared through the glass tanks at the tiny creatures floating near the bottom. It was strange, manipulating these little lives when she had so much trouble with her own.

She sighed and walked to the last tank by the window to get the readings. She couldn't avoid the sight across the plaza. There was the Morrison Planetarium, and there, three floors up, five windows to the right, was Alan's office. They'd thought it was so funny when he was moved into that office, catercorner from her own.

"I'll send messages to you all day long," he'd teased one night in bed. "Smoke signals indicating passion, and big signs in red marker proclaiming my love. Maybe we can string a wire across so if I get desperate I can walk over."

"You're a little long and lanky for a tightrope walker," she'd joked as he kissed her eyes and ears.

"To get closer to you, I'd learn any skill. *And* I'd excel at it."

She stared at the window now, focusing on the spider plant in the center. She couldn't see anyone moving around inside, thank goodness.

After putting her clipboard back on her desk she unsnapped her lab coat and went to hang it in the closet. Her gray turtleneck and slim Black Watch plaid skirt were a little warm in the overheated lab, but as she shrugged on her trench coat and drew the silk scarf around her neck, flipping her ash-blond mane from the collar, she was glad she'd worn wool. It was nippy out, and the late-January damp ate into her bones.

She took a last look out the window as she clicked off the lights. They'd run into each other sooner or later, of course. It was inevitable. Well, she'd just have to be tough and handle it. It wouldn't be so awful if they were in a large group of people.

Yes it would, Kay told herself. It'll be bad no matter what. If only he weren't so close. If only they didn't both work at the institute. Then she could take her time, ease back into things. If only . . . She stopped herself with a short, self-deprecating laugh. If only what happened had never happened and they were going to meet downstairs in the parking lot and drive home to Sausalito to have spaghetti and red wine for dinner and then . . .

She cut herself off with a sigh and slung her purse over her shoulder. Picking up the attaché case with all the work she'd decided to take home with her, she marched out of the lab and down the hall.

There was no one to say good night to. Everyone else had gone home.

"Erica! Help!" Kay shouldered her way through the apartment door clutching her two bags of groceries. Naturally one of them had broken and she was able to stumble into the living room only after two cans of tomatoes and the roll of paper towels rolled in ahead of her.

Erica didn't move much, though, because she was curled up on the couch with the phone wedged between her shoulder and her ear. The expression on her lovely face was absolutely beatific. "Oh, listen, hon, I've gotta go. My sister just walked in. Talk to you later. 'Bye."

She thrust the receiver back onto its hook and finally jumped up to rescue Kay, who had managed to shove most of the errant groceries onto the counter that separated the living room from the kitchen area.

"What's all this?" Erica asked quizzically, picking up a box of chocolate cookies and looking at them in dismay. "You know I never, ever eat sweets." She tore open the wrapping and popped a cookie in her mouth. "Heaven!" she exclaimed, savoring the forbidden delicacy. "Sis, you didn't have to buy groceries," she scolded as she grabbed the intact bag and peered curiously inside it.

Kay laughed and started stacking cans on the one narrow shelf above the pink refrigerator. "Oh, yes I did. Out-of-work actresses may live on yogurt, wheat germ and taco chips, but hungry marine biologists require a little more sustenance."

"You could bring some of your seaweed home to

put on the yogurt." Erica grinned, sneaking another cookie. "Enormously nutritious, I've heard. And really inexpensive. Isn't the whole world going to be existing on seaweed someday when all the soil is depleted?"

"No, only the fish," Kay quipped. "You speak like a person who has never eaten seaweed." She felt better already. Erica seemed to have an uncanny ability to put her mind at rest. It wasn't just Erica's silliness or her vast reservoirs of funny anecdotes. There was something about her—an inner calm—that Kay would have loved to capture for herself.

"I would have cleaned up and washed the floor and hung the curtains like I said I was going to," Erica told her, "but I had a callback for that new play I mentioned this morning. Just a workshop, but they pay for rehearsals."

"Good! How'd you do?" Kay asked, taking the pitcher of iced tea from the refrigerator and pouring herself a tall glass.

"Who knows?" The director was cute, though," Erica commented, reaching for her sister's glass to take a sip. "How was your day?"

"Wonderful." Kay smiled. "It's terrific to have something I have to do. Okay, what do you feel like tonight?" She held up two cellophane-wrapped packages. "Chicken or pork chops? I will astound you with my culinary skills."

"Neither." Erica shook her blond curls. "I'm having Mark."

"What?"

"Mark Sabia!" Erica clasped her hands to her

heart and sighed melodramatically before breaking into uncontrollable giggles at her own performance. "Yummy!"

"Uh-huh." Kay nodded, walking around the counter to take a seat on the couch. "This guy is your latest heartthrob, I suppose."

"Are you kidding? Mark Sabia is the love of my life. My latest? What a horrifying thought, Kay." Erica leaned over the counter to gaze at her sister. "This man is it. The pinnacle. The summit. After Mark, there is no other."

"Sure, sure." Kay laughed. "Too bad. I guess it's chicken breasts for one, then."

"Oh, no." Erica took both packages of meat and tossed them into the freezer.

"Hey, no thanks. I'm not tagging along on your date," Kay said finally. "Just because I'm supposedly your guest is no reason to coddle me. I'll stay home and do my nails, watch a good movie on TV."

"I don't have a TV," Erica said bluntly. "And you're not eating alone."

"Well, then, what am I supposed to do about dinner?"

Erica sighed, putting her hands on her hips in mock exasperation. "You're going to Le Provençal."

"Le Provençal! You must be crazy. Go lie down till it passes." Kay frowned.

"Why don't you believe me? I put together a little surprise party for you at Le Provençal," Erica said, coming around the counter to sit beside her sister. "Guess I spoiled the surprise. I was supposed to smuggle you over there, see, on some pretext or other. Lena and Douglas and David and Beatrice are the party—they've been dying to see you—and me. Except Mark just called. I'm really broken up about this, Kay, but I hardly ever get to see him now that he's with a theater company in Minneapolis. He got a week off in the rehearsal schedule because they switched roles on him, so he flew into town. To see me! Little old me!" Erica clasped her arms around herself and waltzed around the room. She stopped suddenly. "Honest, I'm sorry I ruined the surprise. But it's going to be a fabulous party."

Kay's good mood had vanished by the time her sister had finished her raving. She felt confused and distressed, abandoned out in the cold. Yes, the Villiers and Birches were old friends, very good friends, but she was in no mood for their questions about her three months away, nor could she take any more sympathy.

"What gets me, Erica, is how you could put all this together for me and then just walk away from it," Kay said slowly, her green eyes clouded with annoyance. "If this Mark is going to be in town for a week, then tell him you'll see him tomorrow. You made plans *before* he called."

"Kay . . ." Erica frowned. "I'll take the rap for being somewhat irresponsible, but not for wanting to see Mark. I'm nuts about him, I told you, and this long-distance relationship is an awful drag."

Don't I know, Kay thought suddenly. Being away from Alan for months had been completely unbearable. "You know," she scolded, "you've always been like this with men. When you're alone, you're independent and sure of yourself. But when a man enters the picture you get all weak and mindless. You'd drop anything to come at his beck and call. Remember that guy at college? What was his name? Steve? He had you jumping like a jackrabbit."

"Kay," Erica sighed. "I was a little baby in college. This isn't the same thing. Why are you giving me such a hard time about Mark? You've never even met him. What I really think is that you're scared to go see people who knew you when—"

"That's absurd." Kay got to her feet, more confused than ever. "I'm just annoyed that you feel that this person is more important than the party you set up."

"Okay! All right!" Erica threw up her hands resignedly. "I'm the lowest form of life. Lower than a sea urchin. But I love Mark and this is what I want to do. Now, what do *you* want to do? Stand up your friends? That wouldn't be awfully responsible either, sis."

The two women glared at each other, their unspoken thoughts bouncing around the room. Erica knew that Kay was thinking that David was one of Alan's closest friends. And Lena had known Alan since they were kids together. *I really don't want to go—except I really do,* was written all over Kay's face.

I said I was tough, that I was starting over . . . and I am. "Well . . ."

"C'mon," Erica chided. "You know how impossible it is to get reservations at that place, and honestly, how could the best meal and atmosphere in San Francisco be all *that* torturous? Why don't you go get dressed up like a fairy princess and we'll discuss the evil of my ways tomorrow?"

Kay sighed and looked at the floor. She wasn't as angry at Erica as she was at herself. "Okay. I'll go."

"Marvelous! Now, will you go get ready? The reservation's for eight."

Did Kay imagine it, or was there a mischievous twinkle in her sister's eyes? "Yeah, right," she muttered. Then she turned and started for the closet to select something to wear.

Kay stepped out of the cab in front of Le Provençal and paused to look up at the beautifully restored Victorian. Two antique gaslights illuminated the simple brass placard that told those not already in the know that this was a restaurant. The deep dark brown lacquer of the mahogany door and the subtlety of the entrance gave Kay a comfortable feeling. She could never have tolerated one of the loud, festive, flashy eating places San Francisco was famous for.

Actually, now that she was there, she felt better about Erica's surprise. Seeing friends was probably the best method of getting back into the swing of things, and these four people were very dear to her. The fact that they were also friends of Alan's shouldn't make any difference, she thought.

She pushed open the door and entered a tiny vestibule paneled in the same carved mahogany as the door. The young woman in the coat-check booth smiled up at Kay from her magazine.

"Would you like to check your jacket, ma'am?" she asked.

"Yes, please." Since Kay was going to one of the poshest places in the city, she had dressed for the occasion, something she hadn't done in months. In Golden, clean jeans were about as dressed up as anyone got. But tonight Kay had gone all-out. She removed the short evening jacket, done in black-on-black moiré, a gift from her mother for her thirtieth birthday, and handed it to the attendant. The woman appraised her frankly, and Kay could tell that she was impressed with what she saw. Beneath the jacket was a demure red silk dress with a black leaf print, styled with a large collar that buttoned low and off-center, and a swirling full skirt. The belt was wide, black and brocade. She was also wearing the red satin heels she'd had dyed to go with the dress when she bought it for the Astronomers' Ball, a yearly event that Alan loathed and she loved.

The coat-check woman gave her a ticket and pointed her toward the main dining room. Kay tossed her shoulder-length hair back bravely and walked forward, feeling like a soldier going into the thick of battle. She gave the short, impeccably dressed maître d' Erica's name, and he led her past the bar and into the elegantly appointed restaurant. More than a few heads turned as Kay followed the man to her table.

He led her through a graceful archway decorated with cherubs to a smaller room on one side. Kay was struck by its tasteful decor—pink and beige banquettes, one white rose in a bud vase on each table beside a small lamp that gave off a warm pink glow. The room bespoke intimacy and romance. Kay immediately thought to herself that Alan would love it there. It was just his kind of place. Every once in a while, when he deemed it necessary, he'd "make a surprise," as he used to call it, planning the most romantic evening imaginable and springing it on Kay without warning. Once it was popcorn and red wine in front of the fire in a tiny cabin in the woods he'd managed to get for one night; once it was a Hungarian restaurant with a private room just for them, and a Gypsy violinist right outside the door where they could hear him, but he couldn't see them. Alan was so thoughtful, so marvelous about understanding just what Kay wanted and when she wanted it.

Putting Alan out of her mind, she followed the maître d' until he came to a small table with a Reserved card lying on it.

"This is Erica Rogers' table?" she asked.

"Yes, madam."

"But it's just a table for two. There were supposed to be six of us and she just changed the reservation to five," she told him.

"And I changed it again." The sound of that voice made her heart stop beating for a moment. Then it began pounding so loudly that she was certain everyone in the restaurant could hear it. She turned to face Alan with a gasp.

His craggy face was full of caring and concern. She drank in his appearance like a heady wine, taking in the sight of his unruly curls and well-trimmed beard, his tall body that dwarfed nearly everything around it. He was wearing a navy blazer with antique silver buttons, a starched white shirt, a red knit tie and gray slacks that emphasized his long muscular legs.

But it was his eyes that compelled her the most. Those deep brown eyes set above high cheekbones spoke to her with a language that only they had shared. When she looked into them the rest of the people in the place vanished, and she and Alan were alone. For an instant they stood there on either side of the puzzled maître d', neither one able to move a muscle.

"Madam?" The maître d' cleared his throat and started to pull out her chair, but Alan reacted even more quickly. He took the chair and lifted it away from the table.

Kay just stared at it.

"I will . . . ah . . . return to take your order for drinks in just a moment." The maître d' backed away from them, sensing that something was going on that he wanted no part of.

"Why don't you sit down?" Alan whispered.

"I . . ." Kay's body was completely out of control. She wanted to fight her feelings, the powerful desire both to stay with him and to escape him at the same time. It was too much all at once. Every time she saw him, even heard his voice, she melted like an ice cream in the sun.

"Please, Kay." His deep voice interrupted her thoughts. "Don't run away from me anymore. Come on, just sit down for a second."

She did as he told her because she couldn't even think for herself. As he helped her back in toward the table, she caught a whiff of his after-shave. It was the only one he'd used since she had bought him his first bottle when they began dating nine years earlier.

"Well, I must say you're breathtaking," Alan said solemnly.

She looked at him, suddenly shy, as though this were their first date and they had to go through all the rituals of getting to know one another. "Thank you," she said awkwardly.

"I'm really glad to see you, Kay. You don't know how glad."

She bit her lip. "So there never was any party? You and Erica just cooked this up?" As fearful as she'd been about her first real meeting with Alan after their separation, she couldn't deny that she was glad it had happened this way, that she'd simply been plunged into it like a cold bath.

"No, there really was a party planned for you. I called them and told them it was canceled. I didn't want to deceive you, but your sister said it would be absolutely necessary. You know how overly dramatic she can be."

Kay didn't answer, her silence confirming the fact that she probably wouldn't have come if she'd known he was going to be there. But now she was glad he was.

He looked at her sharply, and she realized how much he cared. The color rose to her face and she began babbling, just so there would be words between them to cover the silence. "Did Erica tell you when my bus was coming in the other night?" Kay asked. "She said she didn't."

"That's true. It was Katherine. She called me the minute you walked out the door. That mother of yours!" He laughed, a wonderful rich laugh that came from deep within his chest. His eyes crinkled up and those long-lost dimples appeared in place of the lines on either side of his strong mouth.

Kay couldn't resist. She started laughing too. "Mom's really something! I think moving into an apartment has affected her brain."

"God, it's good to hear you laugh!" He reached out to take her hand, but she drew back suddenly. The camaraderie that had existed for a moment between them vanished in a flash, to be replaced by an embarrassed awkwardness.

"Well, Lena must be furious about you canceling the party," Kay muttered. "You know how she is about having her plans disrupted. And Beatrice—"

"They all understood perfectly, Kay."

"Oh." Why was she blaming him? Or Erica, for that matter? She was wildly, deliriously happy to be near him again, to sit as they always had, on either side of a table, sharing a meal, an evening. But what if he brought up the tragedy? She could talk about anything else—love, sex, politics, parents, but not what had split them apart.

Just then the maître d' returned, glancing furtively at the two of them as he handed Alan the leatherbound wine book. He seemed surprised to see them both still sitting there.

"We'll have a bottle of this Cabernet Sauvignon," Alan said quickly, pointing, more to get the man out of the way, Kay suspected, than because he was really interested in that particular wine. "And don't bring us the menus for a while."

"Yes, *monsieur.* But of course." The maître d' disappeared and they were alone again.

"Your mother says it's been good having you around the past few months," Alan began softly.

"Yes, it was important for me, too. Well, you know that. She's a bit of a nag, but we did a lot together, and that was nice." Kay felt the strain of this chitchat wearing on both of them. There were so many important things, gigantic topics to bring up, yet they circled the real issues like prizefighters in a ring. There was the reason for her coming back; there was their marriage; there was her friendship with Johnny Pallas. Above all there was the tragedy that hung over them.

"You two get a lot of talking done?" Alan asked, fiddling with his knife and fork.

"Too much. Not enough. Oh, Alan, I don't know," she said testily.

His eyes narrowed. "You'll talk to your mother and sister about it, but not to me. Do you know how that makes me feel?"

"I'm trying not to hurt you," she objected.

"Well, try again, lady!"

They both glared at each other, and the wine steward chose that moment to bring their bottle and uncork it. Kay took a few deep breaths and watched with blind eyes while the steward withdrew the cork, gave it to Alan to sniff and then poured a small amount into his glass.

"That's fine. Excellent," Alan murmured after tasting it.

The man poured them each a full glass and then made his exit.

"I want to propose a toast," Alan said evenly, raising his glass. "To new beginnings."

"To new beginnings," she repeated. They both took a sip of the dark ruby wine and set down their glasses.

"Kay, stop avoiding it," Alan said quickly. "We have to deal with it—together."

"I don't think this dinner is such a great idea," she told him, pushing back her chair. "If you'll excuse me . . ."

"I will not!" His voice rang through the small dining area and several people looked over, astonished, as he grabbed her wrist and yanked her back into her seat. His hand on hers burned like a brand, and when he finally released her, she could still feel the imprint of his fingers.

"I don't want to go through all this again," she murmured.

"That's just too bad, isn't it? You can't shut out the pain, Kay. And you can't shut me out. You're such a scientist, you know that? You think that you can take a problem and devise some experiments and run tests and collect all the data and come up with a solution. So analytical, in perfect control of every situation, minus feelings."

She listened in growing rage to his description of her. "How dare you say I have no feelings? How can you even suggest that?"

"Because we're so much alike. I was guilty of the same thing. Oh, I went about it a little differently from you, but when you left me I locked myself in the observatory every night and worked myself silly. Can't you guess how I tried to wipe the whole slate clean? Well, we can't do that," he continued in a shaking voice. "Nobody can. This lousy time without you has made me stop staring up at the stars through my telescope and start thinking about what's down here on earth. I've only got so much time, Kay, and so have you. We mustn't squander it."

She gazed into his eyes and saw her own grief mirrored there. For the first time since the tragedy she saw Alan as separate from it, a whole human being, not just a part of her own problem. She really had been selfish.

"I need time," she murmured, shaking her head. "More time to think. I'm scared."

"So am I." His eyes flashed with passion for her and with the truth of what he'd said. "Believe me, so am I. But it's always better to be scared with someone else than alone."

In that moment they connected. It wasn't as if the pieces fell into place, of course, but at least they were all laid out in front of them.

I really think I didn't give him credit for having his own pain, Kay thought with a new twinge of guilt. I could only see him as part of my agony. But he's not me, he's my husband, another human being.

Husband. This handsome man sitting across the table was joined to her by bonds that . . . How did the phrase go? "That no man could put asunder." They had vowed to stand together in sickness and in health, in joy and in sorrow, until death parted them. And it almost had.

"Let's not discuss it right now," Alan suggested.

"Let's just sit in the same room, have a lovely meal, take a drive afterward. Let's see if we can manage the simplest things about our relationship. How about it?"

There were tears in her eyes. "I suppose."

"That's all I wanted to hear. That's about all I'm up for tonight, anyway. Shall I get us some menus?"

"I'm not very hungry," she replied.

"Neither am I. I just want to be with you."

This time, when he took her hand she didn't pull away. When the waiter came over several minutes later he found them sitting there, their fingers intertwined, holding on to each other for dear life.

Chapter Four

"How's the veal *à la crème?*" Alan asked, looking at her nearly untouched plate.

"Fine, I'm just—"

"Not hungry, I know." His trout *amandine* had only a few small bites taken out of it. "This is really lousy. I hear the food in this place is the best in the city. We're just not in the mood to appreciate it. Well, some other time."

She looked up sharply. Could there be another time? Of course there could—and there would. Even though she had been on edge all evening, ready to bolt at the slightest provocation, she was happy to be there with him. It felt right somehow. As if they'd put the key piece into place in the jigsaw puzzle.

"How about some dessert?" he asked quietly when he noticed that she was staring into her plate.

"No, thanks."

"Coffee? Espresso? Maybe a liqueur."

"Alan, honestly, I'm finished." She looked up into his eyes. "I've had enough."

"Not nearly enough," he whispered, and his voice was full of meaning. He signaled the waiter for the check, and they sat anxiously, as if waiting for something to happen.

He paid, then collected her jacket from the hat-check woman. Kay noticed the woman staring at Alan, and she read the open admiration in the woman's face. It was true. She had just had dinner with the most devastating man in Le Provençal.

They waited in silence for the valet to bring the car around to the front. Kay did a double-take when the maroon Subaru station wagon pulled up before her. She could remember the day they'd bought that car and the funny guy in the lot who'd promised them that it had only been driven to church on Sundays by the ubiquitous little old lady. Since the mileage was low and their mechanic said the car was in good shape, they had paid the ridiculous price the man was asking.

"Shouldn't we try to bargain him down?" Kay had whispered behind the guy's back.

"Sweetie, I'm an astronomer, not a wheeler-dealer. Anyway," Alan had said, draping an arm around her slim shoulders, "the seats flop down into a bed. Won't *that* be nice?"

And they had taken advantage of that factor that very afternoon, tucked away in a secluded nook on a deserted road, hugging and kissing and making out like teenagers. Kay never failed to be astounded when her husband's serious, intellectual side dropped away to reveal the wildly passionate man who was able to bring her to a frenzy in no time.

Memories flooded her as she climbed inside the car, savoring the familiar smell. It was just like it had been for them in the past, going out to dinner or parties or evenings with friends, and then relishing their review of what had gone on as they drove home to Sausalito. That was always the best part of the evening, Kay remembered. It wasn't that they liked to gossip about people—it was simply that she and Alan agreed on everything and got a kick out of sharing their mutual opinions after the fact.

After the tragedy, of course, all that had changed. Oh, they went through the motions, but it felt wrong, mechanical, as if a bomb had exploded between them, sending them hurtling to opposite sides of the universe. And because it had been so perfect between them before that, the change was devastating.

"It's raining," Alan said awkwardly when they'd been driving for a while in silence.

"I hadn't noticed," Kay responded. What now? This was so stupid! Maybe she should just offer to get out and walk!

Naturally, after he'd mentioned it, she could think of nothing else but the sounds of the rain. The afternoon when they'd bought the car, when they had made love so joyfully in the backseat, it had been raining, and they had huddled closer together for warmth. "Nothing like being cozy inside a car when it's raining," Alan had whispered, running his tongue along the outer rim of her ear.

"Except sitting in front of a fireplace," Kay had objected.

"Maybe we can have one installed in here," he'd suggested before pulling her back down and kissing her all over, from her neck down to her toes.

Now, riding along so far away from him on the passenger side, Kay was embarrassed by the sounds of the windshield wipers and the tires slushing along on the wet road, because they emphasized the lack of communication between them. She wanted to speak, but not a word would come from her parched lips. It was awful to sit like that in dark silence, traveling together but not touching, like parallel lines.

"Well . . ." Alan cleared his throat and pulled over to the curb. Through the smeared window on her side Kay could see the lights of Union Street restaurants and shops, some still busy even at that hour. They were parked in front of Erica's small apartment house. End of the line.

She didn't want to get out of the car, or maybe it would have been more truthful to say that she couldn't move. She needed his presence, his smell, the return to his life and his open arms. After an interminable moment Alan reached over and put his hand on top of hers. She let it stay there, cherishing the warmth that radiated from him. It flooded her body, unexpectedly touching her deep within and making her yearn for him, for what they'd had before. More than anything else in the world she wanted to embrace him, to hold him so close that he would never be parted from her again.

But she was still unable to move toward him. As

much as she longed for him, she couldn't face up to it. She couldn't even grip his hand. Instead she turned to open the door.

"Thanks for dinner," she blurted, betraying everything that was in her heart, everything she should have said, then jumped out of the car.

Alan only sighed, moving his hand back onto the steering wheel. He didn't look up as she closed the door and walked the short distance in the rain to Erica's door. He hadn't asked when—or if—he could see her again, Kay realized as she let herself in. But that didn't matter—it was going to happen. It had to.

She climbed the stairs like a ghost, feeling empty and alone as both bitter emotions and sweet memories swirled through her.

Life was wonderful with Alan, wasn't it? she asked herself. He was always so strong, so there for her. Why didn't she just take what he was offering and stop thinking about it?

It wasn't because she felt she didn't deserve it, not at all. One thing Kay could honestly say about herself was that she was no martyr. The reason their relationship had been so special was that both of them made it that way. Their marriage was a unique pairing of two souls that were truly linked. But her soul had been damaged, eaten away to a few small shreds. As for his, well, she couldn't be sure it fit with hers anymore.

Without even thinking where she was, Kay switched on the light in Erica's apartment.

"Oh, phooey!" Erica squealed, blinking in the bright light.

"What timing!" exclaimed her male companion, intricately entwined with Erica on the sofa.

Kay frowned at the scene she'd interrupted and was suddenly chagrined. There were Erica and her boyfriend, both wearing patterned Japanese kimonos, sprawled together partly on and partly off the sofa. His head was in her lap, and two half-filled wineglasses sat nearby on the coffee table. The remains of a small feast—bread, cheese, pâté and a big bowl of fruit—sat beside the glasses.

"I didn't expect you so soon, sis." Erica giggled, unflappable as ever. "Have a nice time?"

"Hi, Kay." The young man in Erica's arms grinned. He was a small, compactly built man with shining reddish-blond hair that flopped over from a side part and a sandy red mustache to match. His eyes were as blue as Erica's and they had a twinkle in them that lit up his devilish face like a neon sign. "I'm Mark Sabia. No, don't ask how I know your name. The Great Mark sees all, knows all." He and Erica burst into paroxysms of laughter.

"I'm sorry. I'll go someplace and come back later," Kay mumbled. She'd never felt like such a fifth wheel in her life.

"Are you kidding? It's raining antelopes out there," Erica grumbled, getting up to go to her sister. "Where are you gonna go?"

"To a coffee shop. I don't know." Kay wrenched away from Erica's casual hug.

"Kay, will you please stay?" Mark asked, making his way over to the kitchen counter. "We'll make you some coffee. I've been dying for a cup all night, but Erica wouldn't give me a second to go make some. She's been keeping me pretty busy." The two kimono-clad figures clearly couldn't keep their hands off each other, and as they kissed in front of Kay, her confused emotions suddenly boiled over.

"I'll bet she has," she growled, turning away.

"Hey!" Erica glared at her with mixed concern and annoyance. "Don't get testy. He only meant—"

"I know what he meant," Kay barked, pushing past them. "I'll go sit in the bedroom until you're through."

"Kay, what is wrong with you?" Erica gasped.

"Well, in the first place"—Kay turned on her sister, gritting her teeth—"your little deception. How could you tell me there was a party when it was really dinner with Alan?"

Erica sighed. "Oh, that. Look, he wanted to come clean, but I told him you'd never show if you knew. Kay, neither of us would ever do anything to hurt you, but we thought it was high time—"

"*You* thought!" Kay exploded. "Why doesn't anyone give me credit for thinking for myself? I'm a highly intelligent woman. I can make my own decisions about when and how to do things. First my mother, then you, then Alan—"

"They were only trying to hurry you along, Kay," Mark said gently behind her. "So you'd snap out of it."

"What business is this of yours?" Kay whirled on him, her eyes flashing. "I don't need some stranger to tell me what to do."

"You do if you won't listen to your family," Erica countered. She took Mark's arm and led him back to the couch. "Hey, sis, nobody can say how long it takes a heart to heal from a wound like the one you got, but one thing is certain. It's not going to get any better if you hole yourself up in your laboratory and avoid the one person in the world who went through hell with you."

"Oh, God." Kay suddenly slumped into the big chair opposite the couch, all the fight draining out of her. "I just don't understand anything anymore."

"That's clear," Mark said cheerily. "Hey, how's the food at Le Provençal?"

Erica gave him a swift poke in the ribs. "What Mark meant to ask was, was it as bad as you make it out to be? Sitting and talking with Alan?"

"It was . . . not easy," Kay muttered.

Mark shrugged. "Maybe next time you should go to the zoo."

"Mark! Will you quit it!" Erica giggled.

Kay suddenly bolted from the chair. "Who are you anyway, mister? I've never even seen you before in my life and you sit here giving me advice and making jokes. What gall!" She'd never wanted to hit someone so badly in her life. She, the controlled, mature scientist who never lost her cool. What was going on with her, anyway?

"Okay." Mark nodded, his attractive face changing quickly from clowning to caring. "I'm a meddlesome jerk with a big mouth. I was just trying to see if I could punch you out of your mood. Better to be angry at me than at my sweetie here." He took Erica's hand and she squeezed it. "Kay, I can see that there are a lot of people who love you and who honestly want to help you," he went on.

"Don't throw their love in the garbage, because one day when you want it, it's not going to be there."

Kay's eyes narrowed. It felt so weird to have this stranger tell her things she'd been telling herself for months. They shouldn't have meant anything at all, and yet his words struck home.

"What do you know about love, anyway?" she asked. "You tell me that, huh? Aren't you the one who's an actor in Minnesota, for heaven's sake? You think it's funny to come breezing out here when you have a week off to sleep with my sister and then take off again a few days later? Is that what you call love? Because if it is, Mark, then it's my impression that you know absolutely nothing about commitment and sharing. How could you possibly understand a relationship in which you share the tragedies as well as the joys? You know what I think?" she went on, her face flushed with intensity. "I think you probably think real love only exists on a stage or in a movie, right? Well, buster, I've got news for you. Real love, real *life,* is a lot rougher than that."

She was breathing so hard that she couldn't go on, although there was so much more inside her. She couldn't remember when she'd been this worked up. After months of burying all her emotions, keeping them tightly under wraps, there she was getting angry at a total stranger. And why was it that every word she said doubled back on her and kicked her in the stomach? She was talking to herself, not to him.

Mark leaned back on the sofa and crossed his legs in front of him, neatly arranging the kimono over his knees. He was completely unrattled by her tirade. "You're all wet, Kay," he told her genially. "Personally, I don't think life is a bummer, so it isn't. No matter what goes on with me, I look at the bright side. That doesn't mean I'm a cockeyed-optimist type; it only means I have the guts and spirit to keep everything in perspective."

They stared at each other for a moment, even shutting out Erica. Kay couldn't get over the fact that someone else had said something like this to her recently. Johnny Pallas in Golden had the same attitude Mark had: "If life gives you lemons, make lemonade." Well, she was trying, but somehow the stuff still came out tasting like lemons. More sweetness, she thought suddenly, that's what I need to get myself going in the right direction. I shouldn't be so vulnerable, so fragile; I should be cheery and accepting of life's promises, the good ones and the bad ones. She saw how different she had become, and she knew Alan saw it, too. Could he still love her, even without the sweetness?

"Sounds like you have a perfect prescription for happiness," she muttered. Suddenly she was enormously tired, as if she'd come to the last plateau before the top of the mountain and just couldn't muster the energy to haul herself the rest of the way.

"Mark's the last person in the world to tell you what happy is, Kay," Erica said softly, settling herself next to her boyfriend on the couch. "He's the original bad-luck kid. But it doesn't seem to affect him."

"I think my luck has changed." He smiled at Erica warmly. "Except for the fact that you live here and I'm currently stationed in the frozen wilds of Minnesota."

"Oh, that!" Erica shrugged it off as if it were nothing.

Kay sighed and looked at the two of them. They did have something that seemed very precious. "Okay, I'm still listening," she said grudgingly. "How am I supposed to put things in perspective? Give me a new attitude." She was determined to listen to him—and really hear what he had to say.

"Right." Mark looked around and his eye lit on the fruit bowl sitting on the coffee table. "Here's a concrete example. The orange is the sun." He picked it up and sniffed its fragrance, then passed it from hand to hand. "It represents each new day with all its possibilities. Let's call it opportunity. Now, this pear"—he picked it up—"is woman. The banana is man, of course. I'd say the key to happiness is balancing man and woman in conjunction with life's opportunities. Like this." Mark threw the orange up in the air and shifted the banana and pear from hand to hand. Deftly he juggled all three without losing a beat. "See, that's all there is to it."

Erica giggled and grabbed him around the waist, causing him to drop the fruit on the floor. "What a philosopher! That's brilliant, sweetie. Isn't it, Kay?" She turned to look at Kay, but when she saw her sister's reaction her face fell.

"No, I don't find that particularly brilliant tonight. Maybe some other time." Kay picked up her jacket and purse and started for the bedroom.

"Kay, would you give him half a chance?" Erica snapped. "Mark's only trying to cheer you up."

"That's the whole problem!" Kay kept her back to them because she felt tears coming. She wanted —oh, how badly she wanted—to enjoy the simple wisdom he offered her, but it was impossible. "What good is 'cheering up' when there are deep problems that have to be faced? Responsibilities to be taken on? Do you two really think life is all peaches and cream? And oranges and bananas?" She gestured at the fruit on the floor. "It's not all cozy nights and juggling acts, you know. It's commitment, maybe marriage and a family—*if* you can hack that. I don't know, I really don't. You two talk about love so easily, but does it really mean anything to you?"

Mark's face clouded with anger. "Now, just a second," he growled.

Erica grabbed his hand and squeezed it hard. "Forget it, Mark."

Kay stood there glaring at them, her stomach clenched in a tight knot. What was she accusing them for? Everything she'd said in her rage was clearly not directed at them but at herself.

Don't I have a sense of commitment? she agonized. Am I too stubborn, too fearful, to own up to it? More than anything she wanted to accept the love that people were offering her—she could feel it like a warm ocean current flowing from her sister, from Mark, and particularly from Alan. She simply didn't feel ready to plunge into that water yet.

Is it only me, she wondered, or is it Alan too? Does going back to him mean committing myself to more pain, more tragedy? Do I really believe it could happen to us again?

"I don't want to talk anymore," she said abruptly. She turned and went into the bedroom, feeling more confused than she'd ever felt in her life.

Kay didn't turn on the light in the bedroom. She paced for several minutes. They were still out there talking, so she'd just have to wait until they fell asleep. All she knew was that she had to get out and walk. Rain or no rain, she needed to breathe. There was someplace she had to go, and it wouldn't wait.

Quickly she stripped off the silk dress and hung it in the closet. She got out her oldest jeans, a thick white rag sweater and her old work boots. Alan loved to tease her about those boots. "Eh, lady, you gonna woik on a construction site?" But they were waterproof and comfortable and she could walk for miles in them. She tied her ash-blond hair back with a bandanna and took her slicker from a peg in the closet. Then she sat down and counted the minutes.

It seemed like an hour before the door closed and the lights went out in the front room, although it was probably only fifteen minutes. Then Kay waited, hoping that Erica wouldn't jump up and corner her on her way out the door. Like a thief in the night, she moved softly from the bedroom to the living room.

She was out the door and down the stairs in no time. The first gust of wind sent a shower of drops into her face and she started off briskly, her hands thrust into the deep pockets of her yellow slicker, the hood pulled up over her head. It felt wonderful to be outside.

Will Erica ever forgive me? Kay wondered. I probably scared that poor guy off. He'll never want to marry into a family that has a kook like me in it. Suddenly she stopped walking. Wait a second. Why do I assume he'll scare off that easy? Why don't I think he has the stuff to handle an angry sister, or a life with Erica, for that matter?

Kay wiped the rain off her face and walked farther, continuing down the huge slope of the Union Street hill. She wasn't being fair, not to anyone. She just didn't give life the benefit of the doubt. Maybe it wasn't as simple as oranges and bananas, but maybe it wasn't as awful as she'd been painting it. Sure, she had a right to grieve, but she also had an obligation—no, a right—to laugh and love again.

She turned the corner onto Van Ness, and the noise of traffic startled her. It was odd to leave the quiet enclosure of Victorian facades with their gingerbread decorations, the tucked-away country courtyards with fountains playing in the center, and emerge on this thoroughfare of commerce and bright lights.

Her destination called her, and she moved faster, heedless of the rain and wind.

She ran up Van Ness, sloshing water everywhere. The Presidio was closed at night, but she knew a way in at Fort Point that would take her right to the marina.

There was hardly anyone around when she reached the bridge toll plaza and crossed over to the statue of the man who'd built the Golden Gate, Joseph Strauss. She turned north and went through the parking lot, hopping over puddles and feeling a rush of excitement course through her, as if she were a kid out by herself at night for the first time.

She raced down the path that led to Fort Point with a sense of freedom.

The Golden Gate was lit up like a diamond archway leading her home. The fog was so thick on the other side that it seemed as if the bridge dropped off into nowhere. But Kay knew what lay on the other side of it because it was a road she had traveled many times, and always, except once, she had traveled it happily. Her blood felt tingly as the rain pelted her face and hair, but she stared straight ahead in the dark, her eyes piercing the fog and seeing beyond it.

There, on the other side, was Sausalito. There was the home she'd shared with Alan for over eight years.

"I don't believe it's true that you can't go home again," she whispered into the rain. "I want to, and I will. Because I love him, and nothing matters except for that."

When she had drunk in the sight with her mind's eye for a very long time, she turned and started back. If Erica woke up and found her gone she'd be worried. After all, Kay thought with a serious smile on her face, she did have responsibilities; to her sister, to her husband and to herself.

Chapter Five

Three days later the phone rang at the office. "Ada?" Kay called as it rang for the fourth time. "I'm up to my elbows in algae—would you pick that up?" Ada didn't answer, and she knew Tommy, her other assistant, had gone down to the administration building to fill out some requisition forms.

"Oh, for heaven's sake," she sighed, picking up the receiver.

"Nice greeting I get," Alan said on the other end.

Kay's respiration rate jumped into overtime. "Oh, hi, how are you?" she asked, thinking that her response to this man—to whom she had been married for years, after all—was really ridiculous.

"Listen, I'm sorry to bother you in the middle of the day, but the bank has been hounding me to turn in the renewal forms for our six-month C.D. I don't know why I forgot about it when I saw you the other night."

Did she hear a laugh in his voice? Because he hadn't forgotten—he just wanted another occasion to see her?

"Since both our signatures have to be on them, I thought it would be easiest if I dropped over and got you to sign—okay? I'll be over in two seconds."

"Alan, I'm really busy." She wanted to see him—oh, how she wanted to! But she looked awful. Her hair needed cutting and she was wearing a skirt she positively loathed. She would give it to the Salvation Army in the morning, she decided. "You could put it in the interoffice mail," she suggested. "I'd get it this afternoon and I'd send it right back."

"Or I could walk over and hand it to you," he said decisively. "Which is just exactly what I'm going to do." He hung up, giving her no opportunity to object.

She stared at the phone. "Oh, my gosh," she gasped, hurriedly drying her wet hands on her lab coat. She had scarcely had time to run a comb through her tousled hair and dab on a little fresh lipstick when the door to her lab opened. Alan had obviously sprinted across the plaza.

"I didn't realize it was raining so hard," she murmured, watching a small puddle form around his shoes.

He pulled off his slicker with a sheepish smile and shook the drops out of his tight curls like a dog after a bath. "It's a monsoon. Could go on for weeks. Then we'd be stranded here." His eyes told her exactly what he'd like to do, right there in her lab, if they were stranded there any longer than a few minutes. "Mind if I dry off for a second?" He hadn't taken his eyes off her for an instant, and she was acutely aware of his gaze as he took in every aspect of her slender form. The liquid brown warmth of his eyes penetrated her clothing, causing her to blush furiously.

"Sit down." She motioned him toward a chair as casually as she could. "I'm here alone—can't figure out where everyone went," she muttered nervously, searching around desperately for something to say.

"I'm glad. I hate seeing you in crowds." He too seemed a little awkward and nervous about being alone again after so much time. In the restaurant, of course, they'd been surrounded by strangers. Now they had nothing to hide behind. They were on their own.

"You brought the forms?" Kay prompted when he came over to stand beside her. He was so close that she could have touched him without even trying. But she didn't.

"Here you are. A little soggy, I'm afraid." He withdrew an envelope from his inside jacket pocket. "I was thinking," he said as she took the forms from him and began looking around for a pen. "Why don't we renew for a year this time? It's so much less paperwork that way."

She hesitated, then shrugged. "If you want." The implication, of course, was that they'd be together for a year—their money, their house, their car, their lives.

"Do *you* want, Kay? That's what I have to

know." Alan's hand rested lightly on hers and a sigh escaped her lips. There was no doubt in her mind, none at all now.

With a clatter of heavy workboots on linoleum, Tommy came barging into the lab. "Those people, honestly," he muttered. "Worse than the IRS. Dr. Devore, I'm sorry I took so long, but . . ." He stopped, aware that he had interrupted something. "Oh, gee, I'll come back later."

"That's okay, Tommy. Alan, this is my new assistant, Tom Hensley. Tom, this is my husband."

She practically choked on the word. To hide her discomfiture she turned to her desk and began busily scribbling her name on the forms.

"Hi," said Tommy, looking completely astonished as he shook Alan's hand. Kay had never mentioned to him that she had any title other than "Dr." in front of her name.

"You'll check the right boxes, won't you?" Kay asked Alan as he picked up his slicker to leave. "That's for a year this time."

"Not long enough," he said as he walked out of the lab. Just before the door swung shut, Kay saw him wink at her.

She got back to Erica's very late, after having dinner by herself at a diner, then walking around until she couldn't walk anymore. The rain was coming down harder, and she could feel the damp seeping through her sensible clothing into her skin and hair. Even the tops of her shoes were wet through, so she removed them outside Erica's apartment door before tiptoeing in.

Her sister was already fast asleep, alone on the

sofa bed. Kay gave her a brief light kiss on the forehead and it took her back to those days in the big house on Elkin Street. The girls had shared a room until Kay was fourteen and insisted on having her privacy. But that hadn't stopped little Erica. Whenever she had a bad dream she'd invariably get up and go to her sister's room—not her parents'—for comforting. They were that close.

Kay peeled off her wet things in the bathroom and hung them over the towel rack. She stood naked, shivering a little, and ran the shower steamy hot. There were some aches and pains that could be eased—if not cured—by the hot shower. She soaped her fair skin and let streams of water run over her back and down her legs. When she closed her eyes she could almost imagine the touch of the droplets as that of her husband. Alan loved to take showers with her, to surprise her just before she was finished washing by pulling aside the curtain. Then he'd jump in and take the soap and start all over again on her body, rubbing her until she couldn't stand not having him inside her. They would make love and forget the time.

She sighed and turned off the water jets, stepping out onto the bathmat to towel herself dry. As she dried her hair she turned and caught a glimpse of herself in the full-length mirror. Reflected back at her was a slim young woman with full, high breasts and a narrow waist that tapered down to thighs that were very long for someone as petite as Kay was. She could see herself objectively now, and she examined every part of her, as she did her specimens under the microscope. Something was missing. What was it?

For a long moment she considered the alternatives, but when the answer finally dawned on her, she wondered why she hadn't figured it out at once. She was missing a man's caring touch, the attention and devotion that Alan used to lavish on her. She remembered that sometimes after lovemaking he would smile proudly.

"You're glowing now," he'd say, and sure enough she could see it in the mirror. There had been a subtle change after she left him—and now she could see the difference clearly. It was like a light had been turned off inside her.

"Well, that's just too bad, isn't it?" she told herself staunchly. "Lots of women do without love for a while. It doesn't damage them, for heaven's sake."

She hauled herself wearily into the bedroom and climbed under the covers, enjoying the sensation of the cool sheets on her warm flesh. Closing her eyes, she willed herself to forget the conversation in her office about getting back together so soon and fall into a dreamless sleep. Naturally that was impossible.

Twenty minutes later she drew on her blue chenille robe and went over to sit in the love seat by the window. The rain streaked diagonally across her line of vision, drawing lines in her mind. Line one: her marriage. Line two: her job. Line three: the tragedy. Line four: her future. The last line was hazy and indistinct, and the others blended together, her turbulent memories swirling in her head like a dust storm.

Her thoughts wandered to the second floor of the Berkeley science library, to the secluded corner table where she and Alan used to study together when they first started dating. The funny thing about that was that they'd met under rather inauspicious circumstances. It was just before exam period, and seats in the library at all hours were at a premium. Kay had made the mistake of leaving her books when she went out to get a cup of coffee. When she returned she found her place occupied by a tall, bearded stranger with incredible brown eyes who was immersed in an astronomy text.

"I'm afraid this is my seat," Kay said politely.

Alan looked up and smiled. "Not anymore."

"Hey, listen," she fumed, suddenly incensed at his answer. "My books were right here. Now, where did you put them?"

"There were no books here when I sat down," Alan retorted. The two of them glared at each other, ready to fight.

But they were both disarmed when Kay's friend Beatrice popped her head around from the stacks. "Oh, *there* you are!" she'd exclaimed. "I've been looking everywhere. Here, I took your books."

Then Kay and Alan had turned to each other and grinned. She stuck out her hand and he accepted it, holding it just a bit longer than necessary in his powerful grip. The next day he'd called her for a date and they were hardly out of each other's sight after that.

They used to sit on either side of that library table, next to the big picture window that overlooked the campus. Kay could remember all the times she'd lifted her eyes from her biology text to find Alan gazing out at the night sky, his feet up on the table, his fingers linked behind his head. She loved to watch him watching the stars. The wonder and curiosity on his face warmed her and delighted her, and as they fell more deeply in love she was astounded to find that same look on his face when he gazed at her.

Naturally, because they always got a kick out of teasing one another, they made up pet names. He would call her "Urchin" for the sea urchins she studied, and she dubbed him "Stargazer" and "Moon Man," names he was proud of, even though he always protested when she used them.

Staring out the window at the rain now, Kay had an image of Alan's wonderful, childlike expression, the Moon Man face that she loved so dearly. How she missed it! It seemed that after the tragedy Alan hadn't done much stargazing. Or was it that she hadn't noticed because she was so wrapped up in herself then? She just wasn't sure.

A gust of wind blew against the window, rattling the pane wildly. It had rained on their wedding day, just like this. She closed her mind to shut out the thought of that day, but the memories wouldn't let her alone, so she gave in and surrendered to them.

It was a perfectly awful early-April day in Golden, with the spring showers acting more like winter squalls. "This is terrible!" Katherine harrumphed. "How can anyone get married in weather like this?"

"Don't ask her, Mom," Erica joked, jerking a thumb at her big sister. She's too much in love to notice."

Kay had no complaints about anything that day. The house, always a Victorian showplace and famous throughout town, looked like a dream vision. The patterned wainscoting, the pressed-tin ceilings, the etched glass on the front door and the stained-glass panels above every first-floor window had a new shine to them—or maybe it was the shine in Kay's eyes that made everything seem more beautiful, full of wonder.

She had decided on a dress that would go with the decor of the house, and Alan had even agreed to rent a morning suit for the occasion. It would be just family and a few close friends, but they wanted it to be perfect in every detail. They wrote their own service and picked the music, which would be performed by a chamber-music quartet from Denver.

Kay had spent weeks whenever she had time free from classes looking for the perfect wedding dress. It had to be marvelous, ethereal, and yet it had to look real, not like a costume. She must have combed every antique shop in the Bay Area looking for this creation, but nothing she found met the qualifications in her mind.

"What in heaven's name are you looking for?" Erica had asked during one long-distance call. She was appearing in a stock company in Portland, Oregon, and trying to evade the moves of her aging roué director. Her final performance was to be the following week.

"It has to look like something a young woman would have worn at the turn of the century, but you know, sis, a smart young woman—not some flibbertigibbet who liked flounces and too many frills."

"Oh, I get it." Erica laughed. "A young woman just like you. Well, if I run across any hundred-year-old marine biologists with wedding dresses in their trunks I'll be sure to let you know."

Naturally Erica had found the dress. "It's your size and it yelled 'Kay's wedding dress' at me, so I bought it. And it's not returnable, so you'd better love it," Erica had finished, removing yards of pink tissue from around the cream-colored creation in the box.

This was the dress, no doubt about it. Kay gasped when she saw it and hurriedly tore off her clothes so that she could try it on. It was better than she'd imagined it, actually, so perfect that she wanted to cry. The dress was simple but elegant, made of ivory cotton voile and Irish lace. The neck was low and square-cut with an insert of lace that was matched at the edges of the three-quarter sleeves. The bodice fit tightly, with dozens of tiny tucks marching across the front, down to the waist, which flared out gently and fell in three tiers, each one edged with more lace. The dress stopped just at the ankle and closed down the back with nearly a hundred infinitesimal buttons and hooks. It was the sort of dress Kay's imaginary turn-of-the-century woman would have adored, and Kay adored it, too.

And the amazing Erica produced not only the wedding dress but also costumes for the entire wedding party. A good friend of hers from UCLA was now the costume mistress of a Hollywood production company, and she'd agreed—in a pact which Erica swore she'd had to sign in blood—to lend everyone a suitable Victorian costume that actually fit.

There were morning suits with tails and waistcoats, butterfly collars and spats for Alan, his father, his brother, Sam, and Kay's father. There was a variety of elegant gowns for Beatrice, Erica, Katherine and Katherine's sister, Dot. But the biggest surprise of the day was Alan's eighty-two-year-old grandmother, who arrived at the wedding wearing her own mother's wedding dress.

The only one who wasn't in period dress was Reverend Halsey, but no one cared about that. By the time he arrived the musicians were playing and everyone was warming his feet by the parlor fire. The reverend had shaken off his wet trench coat, gathered the group before him. Then, when the first notes of Mendelssohn's Wedding March sounded, Kay had descended the wide front stairs.

What a day that was! she recalled with a small smile. The gusts of wind rattled the old windows and threatened to drown out Reverend Halsey's service. He kept clearing his throat, trying tc talk over the din of the storm.

How like Alan to have stopped the proceedings. In his direct, practical manner, he'd looked around the group and asked for a matchbook.

"I don't have time right now to do a major repair," he had quipped with a loving glance at his bride, "but if I stick a couple of matchbooks in the frame, it'll stop the commotion." Everyone laughed, even the rather somber minister, and as soon as Alan collected a few matchbooks and stuffed them in between the window and the frame, the ceremony continued.

Kay sighed and rubbed her hand across the frosted window so she could see out. It was hard, dredging up all those memories of her past, because the more she thought about it, the more she blamed herself. How could anyone not love somebody as direct and unpretentious as Alan? Most people would have let the window rattle because it was impolite or unconventional to interrupt a wedding service. But Alan went directly to the heart of the matter and took care of it, no matter what protocol demanded. He never let things fester —he believed in attacking problems immediately.

Unlike me, Kay thought with a rueful shake of her head. I'm not a confronter. I just sit there and hope the problem will go away.

And that was why she'd left him. He could confront their tragedy; she couldn't. Or wouldn't.

Had they really been the perfect couple, as Erica and everyone else insisted? "You're so romantic together," Lena had once said to her. "Like your marriage is one long honeymoon." And it had been, until the tragedy. Just as good as the Mexican honeymoon that had started off their life together.

"But I've never even heard of this place, Alan," Kay insisted as the plane touched down at Mexico's Ixtapa/Zihuatanejo airport.

"I assure you, my sweet bride," he said with a smile, depositing a kiss on the tip of her nose, "we are discovering this place before masses of tourists invade it. It's going to be very exclusive in a few years—thank God it's just a fishing village now."

The minibus drove them down rutted roads,

across a small plaza lined with tiny shops and finally out toward the sea. Kay gasped as the panoramic view opened up before her.

"See?" Alan murmured.

"You were right—as usual."

Exactly at dusk the bus deposited them at the back entrance of a small inn called Los Amigos, a pretty enclave of small detached stone cottages around a central building and swimming pool. There were flowers everywhere, and their fragrance filled the air.

"Where did you ever hear about this place?" Kay demanded as the bellhop showed them to their rooms. "I can't wait to get out my filters and test for acquatic life!" She brushed away a large, buzzing mosquito and squeezed her husband's arm in delight.

"Oh, no," he warned her. "The only work that gets done around here is stargazing. You, me, the constellations and a large pitcher of tequila sunrises."

They had drinks and dinner on the outdoor patio, then strolled along the beach, listening to the sounds of the surf and holding each other close. Kay and Alan had practically lived together for the past year, although Kay had kept her apartment "for sentimental reasons," but their decision to marry had brought them closer, somehow. When they retired to their luxurious king-size bed under a slowly revolving ceiling fan at about midnight, Kay was overcome with a deep emotion she had never felt before. When she looked at Alan's strong, muscular form tenderly bending over her, she wondered whether it was right to be so happy. Their naked bodies were lit only by moonlight. That was all they needed.

But as he moved to kiss her a gigantic mosquito flew in between them and went straight for Kay's neck.

"Oh! Unfair!" she squealed, slapping at it.

"Pay no attention. The bugs are naturally hungry after the rainy season." Alan tried to distract her by nibbling the inside of her elbow, but it was impossible. The creatures just wouldn't let them alone.

"This is rotten, Alan," Kay said, swiping at one and missing. "You know I have the sweetest blood in the western hemisphere. These beasts are as big as bees, for heaven's sake."

Alan would not be deterred. He nuzzled the nape of her neck, making the little hairs stand up at attention. "Hey, you, I want you to concentrate," he whispered in her ear.

"I'm trying," she moaned. "But I itch!"

"All right. You asked for it." With that he swept her up in his arms and lifted her off the bed, starting for their tiled bathroom.

"What are you doing?" She giggled in halfhearted protest. "Put me down."

"I am your husband, this is your wedding night and I deserve more attention than the dumb mosquitoes," he said firmly, depositing her in the wide sunken bathtub.

"Alan!" she squealed as he dumped an entire bottle of calamine lotion all over her.

"I'm taking the itch away." He knelt beside her

and began rubbing the pink liquid up her legs and thighs, not missing an inch of her, each stroke of his hand making her yearn for more.

"I don't think you succeeded," she rasped hoarsely, her breath coming in short gasps. "I itch somewhere else now."

She reached for him, but he held her off, making her wait. He covered her stomach with the lotion and rubbed it up toward her breasts, taking her rosy nipples between his fingers and lavishing attention on them. They were immediately erect, and a sigh of pleasure escaped Kay's lips as she arched toward him.

"Would you please get in here?" she begged. He climbed over the edge, and they found that the wide tub was just big enough to accommodate them both. Moving over her, Alan rubbed his body on hers until the dark hair of his broad chest was flecked with calamine.

"Now it's my turn," she whispered wickedly, reaching above him for the spigots. Before he could stop her, she got a grip on one and turned it. Instantly they were drenched as the cold-water faucet spurted on.

"You urchin!" he yelled, dragging her to her feet and holding her against the tiled wall so she wouldn't slip. "Going behind my back!" But then he covered her mouth with his and she tasted the cool water that fell from his mustache. Reaching around him, she drew him toward her so that their bodies were pressed tightly together. She felt his own excitement increase and it excited her to realize that she had such a strong effect on him. He kissed her gently, then roughly, his tongue exploring her mouth and filling her with sweet waves of desire.

When she could stand it no longer he slipped inside her and they rocked together, still holding the wall for support. This man was her husband, she realized in that moment. Her lover, her friend, and now her spouse. As they had linked their hands and hearts in front of family and friends, so they were now linked—forever.

The rain had subsided at last and only a patter of drops against the pane reminded Kay of the storm that had passed. She squinted over at the clock on the bedside table. Four-thirty.

Oh, Lord, I'll never be any use to anyone tomorrow. She sighed, rubbing the bridge of her nose. Why couldn't she be the scientist Alan had accused her of being and control her emotions?

They moved into Alan's tiny apartment in Sausalito and buckled down to work as soon as they got back from their honeymoon. Alan would be defending his dissertation in just three months and he had a lot of preparation to do. Kay and Dr. Josephy, her supervisor at Berkeley, were working on a new series of plankton experiments, which meant that she had plenty to do before she'd be ready for the committee to consider her dissertation.

Everyone had warned them that the first months of a marriage were always rocky and that they were putting an unnecessary strain on theirs because of their work, but that never was a problem for Kay and Alan. Instead of being competitive, of playing that my-work-is-more-important-than-yours game, they fought together like comrades in arms, precisely because they were undergoing the same ordeal.

His sense of humor kept them going, kept them believing that they were both going to be Ph.D.'s within the year and that once they had their academic credentials every institution in the world would want to lure them aboard with promises of high salaries and instant promotions.

"And then, my sweet," Alan told her, waltzing her around the kitchen, "we'll have some money. None of this tuna-and-macaroni-casserole junk. I will buy you fresh water pearls and champagne and whisk you away on a night flight to Italy."

"You mean they don't eat tuna and macaroni in Rome?" Kay pouted. "Then I'm not going."

"Plenty of macaroni. And I will personally serve you tuna in bed," he promised.

Going to Europe became their great dream. Neither of them had ever traveled, and they determined to see the world together—Paris, London, India, Africa and especially Italy. In preparation for the journey they listened to Italian opera while they made dinner each evening, and Alan taught himself to cook just the way they did in Rome and Naples. Their kitchen in that small apartment was always permeated with the mixed aromas of basil, oregano and garlic.

"But what are we really going to do?" practical Kay would invariably ask as they sat on either side of the kitchen table, eating spaghetti and drinking inexpensive red wine by candlelight. "The job market's so lousy, hon, especially for academics like us. One of us should have married a stockbroker."

"Not me," Alan protested fiercely. "I love you for yourself and for your profession too, Kay. You wouldn't be the same if you weren't a marine biologist."

"I guess," Kay admitted feebly. "Dr. Josephy says I can stick around with him until I get my degree, but there's no guarantee they'll need someone else on staff. Maybe some small college in northern California will be interested. I'll get a list from somewhere. I was also thinking of sending résumés to all the vineyards. Maybe they'll need another hand in the labs."

"Darling, winemaking, like lovemaking, is chemistry. What do you know about chemistry?"

"I'll learn," she declared hotly.

They each mailed out fifty résumés, taking nothing for granted. The only thing they never considered was applying outside of northern California, because their only criterion was that they never be separated, and if one of them got a job locally, while the other had an offer from far away, they would have to confront that issue.

Just for the hell of it, they both put in applications at the California Academy of Sciences in Golden Gate Park. Kay's exact words as they dropped their letters in the mailbox were, "It's like applying to Harvard. You know you'll never get in, but you have to apply because everyone does."

The next few months were totally crazy. Kay and Alan were at the library more than they were at home, and because of Alan's work he had to be at the observatory each night to make calculations. He'd arrive home at three or four A.M., stumble into bed, wrap his arms around his sleeping wife and drift off. During the final weeks before their orals Kay nearly panicked. There just wasn't time —time for cooking, or lying in bed in the morning, or studying, or making love.

Nothing could have been more welcome than the letter that arrived for Alan two days after he defended his dissertation. "I can't open it," he moaned when he saw the Morrison Planetarium letterhead. "I'm so tired I wouldn't be able to read it. Go ahead." He pushed the letter into her hands and she trembled as she opened the envelope.

"'Dear Mr. Devore,'" she began. "'We are pleased to inform you . . .' Oh, Alan, they want you! You've got the job. Oh, wait a second, 'contingent on your being awarded the degree of doctor of sciences from Berkeley.' You got it! You did it!" She shrieked, jumping at him and covering him with kisses. "I knew you would."

It was this pride in each other that kept them from celebrating until Kay had heard something about her possibilities. The odd thing was that she wasn't jealous about Alan's success, or that he'd heard first. No, she was just anxious that she wouldn't end up with something too far away. So when her letter from the Steinhardt Aquarium arrived the following week they both dissolved in delirious laughter.

"What'd I tell you, partner? Good things come in threes—first our marriage, then my job, then yours."

"I can hardly believe it," Kay marveled, kissing her husband for about the hundredth time that hour. "What do we do to celebrate?"

"Let's see . . ." Alan grinned, sitting down on their dilapidated sofa and drawing Kay onto his lap. "On my list is buying a cozy little house with a view of the water right near here, replacing this awful piece of furniture"—he thumped the sofa cushion for emphasis—"and picking out those freshwater pearls I've been threatening to buy you. But for today, how about the zoo?"

So they went racing like children from one cage to the next, commenting on how the raccoon looked like Dr. Josephy and the way the elegant snow leopard reminded them of Erica in a serious moment. They waited for the lions to be fed and then moved on to the merry-go-round, where they straddled two horses and held hands as the calliope began playing.

"I have another great idea for the future," Alan said to her while he went up and she went down.

"Aw, you never run out of ideas. What's new about that?" she called over the loud music.

"I was thinking about a baby."

She glanced over at him, a mischievous smile on her face. "You were, huh? And who's going to take care of this baby while I'm with my urchins and you've got your eyes glued to a telescope?" Actually, she was pleased that he'd brought it up. They'd talked about having children several times during the previous year, but neither of them had mentioned it lately.

"That's the great thing about an academic schedule." Alan laughed. "And Jeannie Wharton, the professor who's just started working at Morrison, mentioned that she leaves her eighteen-month-old in the nursery at the administration building when she and her husband are working. It'd be perfect for us."

"I'm glad you have it all planned, Dr. Devore." She'd smiled down at him as he lifted her off her painted horse. "But don't you think we should settle into our new jobs first?"

"Oh, all right, if you insist." They linked fingers and walked out the gate together. "But let's not wait too long, okay?" he said.

"Fine with me." They exchanged a long look, one of love and commitment, one that promised a long bright future.

"Now, what about that celebration dinner?" Alan suggested at last, breaking the serious mood. "I know for a fact that this zoo has the best hot dogs and sauerkraut in San Francisco. And then"—he pulled her close—"back home for champagne in bed."

They walked down the path toward the refreshment stand, their hearts so full that they felt like singing. *Life is really wonderful*, Kay marveled. *And so are we.*

Kay drew back from the window, tired at last, so exhausted from the past hours of thinking that she could scarcely drag herself to the bed. The sky was getting light by then, its gray shroud lifting to reveal the colors of the new day.

But for Kay it was finally time to put her memories to rest. When I wake up, she told herself, I'll have some answers.

She put her head down on the pillow and fell at once into a quiet, dreamless sleep.

Chapter Six

"Would you check those test tubes, Ada?" Kay asked, barely looking up from her microscope. "I think they should be ready."

"Sure, Kay, I'll pull them out." Ada Ortiz strode out of the lab, leaving Kay with Tommy.

"Tommy," Kay asked him, "have you done a temperature reading on the tanks today?" She peered at him wearily over her microscope, her vision adapting gradually. Her eyes felt sandy and puffed—was it possible that she was working herself too hard? She'd have to watch it. Since that rainy night, Kay had made a conscious effort to submerge herself in her work. She hadn't even bothered to go apartment hunting, since sometimes she slept on the couch in her office.

"Uh, no, Dr. Devore, sorry," the young man apologized. "I'll do it right now."

"These things are vital, Tommy. Please remember. Sea urchins may be insignificant to the American economy, but they're really important to Ada and me."

He gave her a nervous smile and went over to check the tanks. Kay bent her head back over her microscope. There was nothing to it, really. Work was absorbing; it was healing. Concentrating on work and nothing else was good for her, like taking a vitamin every day, strengthening and preparing her for the ultimate test—returning to Alan and facing their problem.

"Dr. Devore, I'm sorry to bother you, but this gauge is all off. I think we'll have to call someone in to fix it," Tommy told her. "The water doesn't feel anything like the temperature reading."

"Oh, great," Kay muttered. "That means we have to chuck today's printout. Look, you take care of this, would you? I'm due at a meeting." She glanced annoyedly at the incorrect data and shook her head. "Hey, it's not your fault," she said to the distraught technician. "Don't look so glum."

"Thanks, Dr. Devore." His thin, serious face lit up for a moment. "I'll see that it's fixed by morning."

"Great." Kay walked out of her lab, grabbing her notebooks and clipboard. If only it were that easy, she thought to herself. Just tell yourself it wasn't your fault and you can start all over tomorrow.

She sighed and walked down the steps to the first floor, then hurried across the plaza in the brisk wind to the administration building. She wasn't really in the mood to sit around and listen to everyone discussing staff woes, but what could she do? It was all part of academia.

The first floor of the building was humming with activity as Kay went through on her way to the elevator. The door opened and she walked in with several other scientists who were having a heated discussion about the annoying frequency of interoffice memos.

Oh, marvelous, Kay moaned inwardly. This'll be a doozy of a meeting. Real hot topics.

When she got out on the third floor she let everyone precede her down the corridor. She had somewhere to go first, a place she'd been avoiding ever since she had come back to San Francisco.

The door was gaily decorated with cut-out snowflakes and snowmen—the children's version of what they thought snowmen should look like, since most of them had never seen snow. Kay looked through the window of the nursery, feeling blank inside. Then suddenly the door opened and she was startled to see Maggie Tolan, the director of the day-care center.

"Kay Devore! How *are* you! I didn't know you were back." The chunky round-faced woman embraced Kay warmly, and she responded in kind.

"Yes, I . . . I've been awfully busy. That's why I didn't come over to say hi," she muttered, thinking how lame that excuse sounded.

"How's Alan?" Maggie asked.

"He's . . ." Kay started to think up a long, involved explanation and found that her mouth wouldn't form the words. But she didn't have to say anything, because at that moment Alan stepped out of the elevator and walked briskly down the corridor toward them.

"Maggie!" he said, coming over to the woman and kissing her on one cheek. "I've really missed you." He looked over Maggie's head at Kay and his eyes took on a questioning look.

"What are you doing here?" he asked, releasing Maggie. He stared at Kay so hard that she started blushing.

"The same thing you are, I guess," she murmured softly.

"Well," Maggie said with nervous cheeriness, looking from Alan to Kay and back again. "I would love to stand here and chat with you both, but I'm bedeviled by work and more work. Every one of my tots has a cold." She shrugged. "So I'll see you later, okay?" She disappeared behind the door without waiting for good-byes.

"Are you . . . ah, going to the staff meeting?" Alan asked awkwardly.

"Right. And you?" They were standing so close together that they might have been touching, and yet they were distant, even formal, with each other.

"These things are really getting more deadly by the month. You should be glad you missed three of them," he said as they started down the hall toward the auditorium.

Kay had no idea how to react or what to say. Naturally he was referring to the three months she'd been in Golden, but his remark was so casual that it might have been addressed to a stranger. She had the oddest feeling about seeing him there, on that floor, talking to Maggie. She wanted to hug him and hold him, and yet she was powerless to do anything but make small talk.

"Shall we go in?" he offered, holding the door for her.

She knew how difficult this had to be for him because she felt it herself. They walked into the room together and she could feel every eye turn toward them. The staff of all three institutes was present—Steinhardt, Morrison, and the Wattis Hall of Man, where the anthropologists worked. But clearly there were people here who knew all about Kay and Alan, and several with professional gripes or too much competitive spirit who would surely love to gossip about seeing them together.

So what? Kay thought, lifting her head proudly and walking toward a chair. Let them imagine whatever they wanted.

She sat down and Alan took the chair beside her. He crossed his legs as he took a pen from his jacket pocket and accidentally poked her with his foot. She recoiled as if from a hot poker.

"Oh, I'm sorry," he said, too urgently. "Did I hurt you?"

"No, of course not." She laughed. "I'm just touchy these days."

He looked so terrific, she noticed, wearing tan chinos and a white shirt open at the collar under a tan-and-blue tweed jacket. She pried her eyes away from him as the chairman of his department, also an administrative bigwig, came to the microphone and tapped on it.

"Want to cut class?" Alan asked her quietly.

"Alan, we can't miss this. They'd have our heads," she whispered, wishing like anything that she could say yes to him, in more ways than one.

"Okay." He sighed, slumping down in his seat and stretching his long legs out in front of him. "But don't say I never offered."

The meeting droned on, one boring topic following another. When Kay walked out she couldn't for the life of her recall one thing that had been said. All she was conscious of was Alan beside her, his lovely masculine scent filling her, the warmth of his body making her flush. He'd had a haircut since she last saw him, and he looked very neat and boyish, his beard hugging his handsome face and his tight brown-and-silver curls capping his head.

There was something different about him, Kay noticed, but she couldn't put her finger on it. Something stronger and more mature. The tragedy had sent her reeling into self-pity, but it had done something positive for Alan. As horrible as it was, as hard as it had hit him, it had forced him to grow up. She had loved him before for his boyish enthusiasm, but now she found that she was falling in love with him all over again—for his maturity, his patience.

Until I go back to him, she said to herself with a shock of realization, I'm in limbo.

They walked out of the meeting nodding to their colleagues and letting the hubbub of the chatter around them foil any attempts at conversation. They just walked quietly, inches apart, until they reached the elevator with a group of other people.

Suddenly Alan grabbed her hand, making her

gasp. "Let's take the stairs," he muttered, yanking her away.

"Alan—"

But he didn't give her time to say another thing because he was already hurrying her down the hall toward the exit sign. When they had stepped through the heavy metal doors he cornered her in the stairwell, one hand on either side of her, pinning her against the wall.

"When, Kay?" he demanded. "I want an answer."

She met his burning gaze, filled with passion and anger, and she was torn. Gingerly she put a hand on his sleeve. "Soon, I promise." Then, quick as lightning, she ducked under his right arm and fled down the stairs.

It was too late to go back to the lab, and with her thoughts in such turmoil she wouldn't have gotten anything accomplished anyway. She ducked back into her office to get her jacket and a few notes she wanted to go over that evening. Was he waiting for her in the plaza? she wondered. Then she made a face and sank down in the chair behind her desk. Wasn't this cat-and-mouse game getting kind of silly? She felt so ridiculous about it. After all, what was going to happen? They'd sit together, they'd talk it out, probably cry a little, and end up . . . where? That was the hard part, the one question she couldn't answer. Because if they ended up on opposite sides, bickering again, it would be too much for her to handle.

It was nearly dusk as she walked back to Erica's. The shops were closing up and the restaurants getting busy for the cocktail hour. But it was lighter out than it had been the night before at that time. Could it be that spring was coming? She'd hardly noticed the seasons since she came back from Golden. She hadn't noticed all the things she loved about San Francisco, the steep streets like mini-mountains, the cloistered gardens behind little gates, the magnificent span of the Golden Gate, the cable cars clanging their way around town.

Well, she thought, noticing one tiny crocus peeking out at her beside an ornate Victorian on Union Street, I'm not going to miss spring. I'm going to enjoy it.

She was in a very determined frame of mind when she let herself into the apartment a few minutes later. She flipped on the lights and was surprised to see Erica lying on the couch, one arm draped over her eyes.

"Hi, sis." Kay smiled, shrugging off her jacket. "Have I interrupted some method-acting exercise or something?"

"No," Erica replied so quietly that Kay immediately assumed the worst.

"Hey, what is it?" She went over to sit beside Erica. "Are you okay?" She peered at her sister's face in the dim light. "You look kind of green."

"It's my new makeup," Erica quipped, moving her legs aside and sitting up slowly. "Very punk, don'tcha think?"

"Well, that's more like it! For a minute there I thought you were sick or that tragedy had struck."

"Uh-uh. As a matter of fact," Erica said, hugging herself tightly, "it was a banner day. I got all sorts of news."

"Yes? Well, don't keep me in suspense," Kay insisted.

"I got that part I auditioned for last week." Erica grinned. "Finally I'm not typecast. I get to play the *evil* other woman—how about that?"

"Sweetheart, that's marvelous!" Kay yelped, embracing Erica tightly until she noticed that her sister had her head averted and was sort of gasping for breath. "Wait a minute. You *are* sick; you can't fool me. This must be flu or something. All right, you lie down again. I'll make you my famous chicken soup right out of the can. It's about time I took care of you for a change." Kay got up and marched to the kitchen area to scrounge up some supper.

Erica flopped back down and stretched out. "I'm fine, honest," she moaned.

"Sure you are. You probably got so worked up about this wonderful part that you didn't notice you were sick. Okay, tell Mommy," Kay went on, kicking off her shoes and rattling around under the counter for a pot with a cover. "What are the symptoms and how long have you felt this way?"

"Well, nausea," Erica began quietly. "And I haven't been sleeping too well."

"Uh-huh. Sounds like anxiety and exhaustion. I know just what to do." Kay suddenly felt very much in charge, in control of the whole situation. It was good to stop feeling sorry for herself and do something for someone she cared for. In the back of her mind she realized that she would have liked to do something for Alan, to ease his pain, but barring that, there was Erica, and Kay was really happy to have the opportunity to nurse her and coddle her a little. She was reminded of the time just after her father died, about two years earlier. Alan and Erica had been wonderful with Katherine, very supportive and comforting, but it was Kay who got things done. She called the accountant and the bank and the lawyer and took care of a hundred little details that no one else had even thought of. Of course, she was grieving for her father all that time, but being active and helpful seemed to take her mind off the tragedy.

She stopped suddenly, pot in hand. "Oh, no," she said aloud. Was that just another instance of running away from the truth? Did she always handle crises by being blank and busy? For a second she stood there in the kitchen, dumbfounded at this realization. Every time something awful happens, she thought to herself, I get out of dealing with it by being capable and taking care of details. She was so shocked at herself that she almost missed seeing Erica gag and pull herself upright.

"Erica?" she asked.

Her sister put up a hand, then clamped it over her mouth as she lunged for the bathroom.

Kay dashed after her and plucked a washcloth from the side of the basin. Quickly she ran some cool water over it and wrung it out. Kneeling next to her sister, she gently wiped her face. "You want me to call a doctor?" she asked in a concerned tone.

"No, of course not." Erica took the cloth from her, then slowly got to her feet. She leaned against the wall, pressing her head to the cool tiles. "I'm perfectly fine."

"Sure you are," Kay muttered sarcastically. "I could probably discover some new weird physical condition if I did a culture on you."

"It's not a new condition," Erica said, her blue eyes cloudy with discomfort. "It's the oldest one in the book. C'mon, Kay, let's sit down."

They walked back in the living room and Erica nearly fell back on the sofa. "You want to hear my other symptoms? Sore breasts, bloat." She scanned Kay's face. "Shall I go on, or have you guessed?" Erica asked, taking Kay's hand.

Kay shook her head. "What are you saying? Are you telling me you're—"

"Pregnant. Uh-huh. That's exactly it, Dr. Devore. Your diagnosis is as good as my own doctor's. About six weeks' worth." Erica was half-smiling, half-frightened at Kay's reaction.

Kay blanched and her body stiffened. "I didn't know. Pregnant." It was the only thing she could think of to say.

"Pregnant," Erica repeated. "And I have morning sickness in the evening. I usually manage to do things the unorthodox way." Her face lightened as a wide smile spread across it. She pushed the disheveled curls out of her face.

"Mark?" Kay asked.

"Of course. You had to ask?"

Kay blinked and looked at the coffee table. "I remember when I found out I was pregnant," she said in a faraway voice. "Alan was so happy that night. He stood out on the back deck and shouted to the world that he was going to be a father. That was one of the best days of my life. . . ."

Then Kay looked at her sister, worry suddenly creasing her face. "What are you going to do about it?" she asked in a whisper.

"What do you mean, what am I going to do about it? I'm going to have a baby, Kay," Erica said staunchly.

"But you two aren't . . . And he's out in Minnesota, for God's sake," Kay sputtered.

Erica slapped a hand over Kay's mouth. "Wait a second," she barked. "Now, will you please get calm?" She waited a minute, then removed her hand. "Mark and I discussed this long ago, Kay. We planned to have this baby. We're looking forward to it. We might even be good parents. And we timed it pretty well, I must say." She gave her sister a wicked wink.

"Are you out of your minds? What kind of father can he be, working fifteen hundred miles away? Where are you going to put this baby?" She gestured around the tiny apartment. "This is insane!" She got up and stalked over to the sink to pour herself a glass of water.

"Kay, honestly, we've thought it all out. Mark's contract expires in September, so he'll be back here just in time. And once he's here we'll look for a bigger place. He's already got a couple of job possibilities all lined up. He's *very* resourceful." She stopped as another wave of nausea hit her. "If only I didn't feel so ghastly. This puky feeling *cannot* interfere with my rehearsals," she proclaimed, shaking a fist at the silent walls. "It should be over by the time we're in previews, don't you think? It'll be just my luck that the showcase is an enormous hit and somebody decides to book us into a regular theater for a run. I could only stay with the show four months tops. I mean, how can you have an evil other woman who's pregnant? I *ask* you."

Kay stopped pacing, turned and stared at her sister. "I can't believe you! Do you think having a baby is some kind of game? Do you think you can anticipate everything that can happen? Just write it on your calendar and expect things to follow your schedule? How dumb can you get?" Then her eyes narrowed. "Or is this an act—for my benefit?"

Erica sighed and sat up again. "I told Mark you weren't going to take this well."

"How am I supposed to take it?" Kay demanded. "You're not married. Neither of you has a steady job, and he's even intending to give up the job he does have."

"Not 'give up,' for heaven's sake, Kay. I wish you'd listen to yourself. First you criticize Mark for being too far away to be a father. Then he's a louse because he's coming back here after the season's over." Erica got up and walked to her sister, putting her arm around her resistant shoulders. "That's not what's really upsetting you, Kay. You know it and I know it. Look, I've done a lot of reading about this. I even made an appointment and went to see Dr. Teller as soon as my doctor confirmed the blood-test results. They don't think it's genetic, Kay. The chances of it happening to me are pretty remote."

Then Kay started to cry, painful, racking sobs. More than anything she wanted to be happy for her sister because she knew that this was something good and joyful. But part of her held on to the old fears. The thought of her little sister pregnant, then giving birth, holding her own infant in her arms to nurse, seemed so strange to her. Goofy Erica was like a kid herself sometimes. But a great person, too. So why shouldn't she be a good mother?

Suddenly Kay began to laugh through her tears. "We're so different," she said, sniffling a little. "When I was pregnant . . ." She shook her head, letting the sentence trail off. Then she grabbed Erica by both arms and pulled her close for another hug. "You *do* know that I'm happy for you?" she whispered in her sister's ear. "I really am. But I'm scared, too. And I don't know if I'm more happy or more scared."

"You have to help me with everything, Kay," Erica said firmly. "What to eat, how to exercise, what kind of goop to rub on my belly so I won't get stretch marks. Please? Help me."

The sound of the telephone shattered the moment and Kay jumped, feeling a kind of guilty relief that she wouldn't have to talk more about it right away. "I'll get it," she offered.

"Kay," Erica said, "it's probably Mark. For me."

"Hello?" Kay picked up the receiver on the second ring.

"Hello, Kay? Is that you?" Katherine's voice crackled over the long-distance wire.

"Mom! Hi, how are you?" Kay's mind was awhirl with thoughts; she was wondering how she was going to deal with her mother's inevitable questions—and how she should handle Erica's news.

"I'm old and crotchety," Katherine answered in

her typically brusque manner. "How are *you?* That's the crucial thing." Her voice had a sardonic tone to it that made Kay aware she had something on her mind other than chitchat.

"I'm okay." Kay spoke cautiously, taking a seat on the couch. "I'm finally settled in back at work. I'm training a new assistant," she offered, sure that Katherine wasn't at all interested in this information.

"How nice." Katherine brushed it off. "Say, I'm astounded you answered Erica's phone, by the way. You ought to be home by now."

Kay frowned down at the receiver. "Listen, Mom—"

"Time," Katherine interrupted, "is a-wasting, my girl. If you want my opinion, which I know you don't, though I'll give it to you anyway, I think if you ignore him long enough he'll just disappear."

"Mom, it's hard for you to get a good picture of this when you're so far away. Believe me, that's not how it is."

"Then how is it?" Katherine demanded. "Tell me—I want to understand. Kay, Alan is a damn good man, the best I've ever known, next to your father. You used to be so happy together—why won't you give him a chance?"

"Look, Mom, Erica has something she wants to tell you," Kay said, cutting her mother off. "Her news is a lot more important than us rehashing the same old argument all over again."

"It makes me sad to see you like this," Katherine persisted. "No one's trying to deny that you've had more than your share of hurt. What happened to you is the worst thing a woman can go through, but you can't go back now, Kay. You can't act like a turtle and hide in your shell. That's not fair to Alan and it isn't fair to yourself. I remember how when you were little you were always the brave one, Kay, always protecting your baby sister from the small hurts—the bogeyman under the bed, the scary frogs in the pond. Well, isn't that so? Didn't you used to be the brave one?"

Kay stared at the phone, feeling unable to deal with everything her mother was dishing out. "I agree that's so. But things have changed. We all change, you know."

"That's fine—just so long as it's a change for the better."

There was silence, neither of them venturing an opinion about the change in Kay. Then Katherine said, "Now, before you put Erica on the line, I have to bring up another difficult subject. Since you won't discuss your husband with me, let's try your old boyfriend Johnny."

"That's not funny," Kay snapped. "He was never—"

"Oh, all right, not boyfriend, just friend. You sure left me holding the bag on this one, girl. He's over here three or four times a week asking about you. Your absence is definitely making his heart grow fonder. He doesn't realize he was just good therapy for you when you were here, and I haven't the heart to tell him. I wish you'd write him a 'Dear John' letter or something."

"Oh, Mom, I'm sure he doesn't think there was anything between us. How could he?" Kay said, rather chagrined at the thought of Johnny missing her. She didn't want that.

"How do I know? Men are funny creatures, Kay. That boy hurts, and he was hurting when you left. Your problem is that you were so wound up in your own misery that you didn't think twice about what you were doing to someone else. Have a heart, Kay. You used to care about others."

Kay was shocked by her mother's statement. Was she really that unfeeling? And could she have been so lacking in perception that she didn't realize how Johnny felt about her? "I do care, Mom," she whispered.

"Then write him or call him and tell him you have a life of your own in California and that you've worked things out with your husband. Lie if you have to. Don't let this boy go on thinking he can get you back."

"I'm not going to call him," Kay protested. "That would just make him think I was interested."

"Well, I'm not going to turn him down for you. I can't bear seeing his hound-dog face at my door every other day. If you don't get in touch with him soon, I'll tell him where you are."

"Don't you dare!" Kay shrieked so loudly that Erica looked over at her in dismay.

"Then do the right thing!" Katherine harrumphed. "Now, I'd like to speak to my other daughter, if it's not too much trouble. And she'd better not have bad news. What is it she wants to tell me? Some new part in a play?"

Kay took a couple of deep breaths before responding. Her mother could be so infuriating! First the Alan lecture, then threatening her with Johnny and capping it all with not so much as a "Take care of yourself." "Here, Mom. I'll let her tell you herself. And I hope you're sitting down," she finished. Then, cupping her hand over the receiver as she passed it to her sister, she whispered, "She's in a mood tonight. Maybe you'd be better off telling her tomorrow."

"Oh, great," Erica whispered back. "You really are brave, aren't you?"

Kay was stung by her sister's comment. Both Erica and Katherine were really disappointed in her. But perhaps not as much as she was in herself.

"Hi, Mom," she heard Erica say cheerfully. "Guess what?"

Kay counted to three and closed her eyes.

Then Erica continued. "I'm going to have a baby."

Kay could hear her mother's squeak of shock. She ducked under the phone cord and went into the bedroom to change out of her work clothes. But first she stood in the doorway, listening to her sister laughing at something their mother had just said.

"I know." Erica giggled. "But we'll work it out. Isn't it wonderful? I'm so happy!"

Kay closed the door behind her and forced a smile to her lips. It was wonderful, and she would be happy—eventually.

Chapter Seven

Kay stood in the middle of the plaza at the California Academy and looked around. It was early, just after eight, so there were only a few eager-beaver scientists walking past her toward their offices. On one side of the plaza was her favorite sculpture, a large bear hugging its cub; on the other was a big unferocious-looking cat and, in front of the aquarium, a playful dolphin. There was nothing more fun, she recalled as her feet directed her away from her office, than sitting out there for lunch with Alan and watching dozens of children climbing all over the statues, not listening to their anxious parents telling them to be careful.

"We'll never be like that," Alan used to whisper.

"That's because our kid will be a champion climber—not to mention a gorgeous, sensitive, intellectual wonder of the Western world," Kay had responded once.

She sighed and shook her head, walking briskly up the steps of the Morrison Planetarium. It seemed like years since she'd last been in there. She pulled open the door and stepped into the quiet corridor. Then she stopped, unable to follow through with her decision.

"Come on," she told herself aloud, because there was no one around to hear her. "It's time. You've got to go see him." That started her moving. She walked to the elevator and pressed the button, thinking that it would be just her luck for Alan to have decided to come in late that day. Except he wouldn't. She could feel his presence in the building, sense it calling to her.

After the whole thing with Erica the previous night she'd taken a long walk and given some serious thought to her crumbling relationships with everybody around her. Katherine was right, there was no denying it. The three months in Golden had been an easy way to avoid life, and ever since she'd been back in San Francisco she hadn't done a thing to remedy that. Oh, she was a great liar, telling herself she was starting over, getting ready to deal with her husband, picking up the threads of her work just like a well-adjusted, normal woman.

"Hogwash!" she muttered, stepping into the empty elevator and pressing his floor. If she was managing so well, why hadn't she called Beatrice or Lena, her two closest friends? Why hadn't she started the dance class Erica had found for the two of them? Why hadn't she read one good book the way she'd intended to? She couldn't even concentrate on a fashion magazine these days. The only reason she was able to do her serious scientific research was that it came to her almost by rote—she could do experiments and check data virtually without thinking.

No, the real truth was that she was still running away, and now, not tomorrow, not the next day, was the time to quit. Erica's startling announcement had turned her head around, had made her realize that her own period of mourning and self-pity was over. "Good riddance to it," she muttered as she got off the elevator. "It's time to start living again."

She didn't hesitate at all now as she walked toward Alan's office. She felt as though there was a string tied to the center of her forehead, pulling her to her destination. It felt good to be doing this at last, walking down these familiar halls, smelling their old mustiness and reading the name tag on each door.

She came to the end of the corridor and turned down the short hall that led to Alan's office. And suddenly, as she approached it, she saw something she'd totally forgotten about, and her determined expression melted into one of gentle amusement. On Alan's door, under his nameplate, he'd hung a color photo he'd taken of the full moon one October night. It was an incredible picture, the intricately cratered harvest moon a pale golden color against the blue-black night sky. Each wrinkle of its surface made it seem palpable, so close that you could almost believe that its distance from the earth was nothing at all, that it was just around the corner, waiting for you to take a stroll on it.

Alan had written along the bottom edge of the photo, "Up above the moon so high . . ."

Kay paused with her hand on the doorknob and remembered the day almost three years earlier when he'd hung up that picture.

"Wait a second," she had told him with a wry smile. "You've got the lyric wrong. It's 'Up above the *world* so high/Like a diamond in the sky.'"

"Too bad." He had laughed, whisking her inside his office for a quick kiss. "I rewrote it in the interest of scientific accuracy. It's an undebatable fact, Kay, that the stars are thousands of miles farther from *us* than they are from the moon. I think my image makes more sense."

"Yeah, and it goes much better with your picture, too." She'd grinned. "What a coincidence."

Now, as she stared at the photo on his door, she marveled at her memory of the Alan who was whimsical and inventive. Why did she persist in remembering how angry he could get, how demanding he could be? Why, he's like a child himself in many ways, she thought suddenly. I bet Sean would have been just like—

"Kay!"

She turned abruptly to see Alan standing at the end of the hall, holding a steaming cup of coffee. He looked shocked to see her, but delighted, as well. They stood staring at each other until Kay realized that her vision was obscured by tears—tears of joy.

"Alan," she said softly, "I want to talk now."

"Of course. Come on inside. You . . . ah, want some coffee?" He looked almost afraid to come closer, as though he thought she might suddenly change her mind and fly away.

"No, thanks. Really."

"You can have some of mine, then," he offered.

"Alan, I don't want any coffee. Let's go in."

He nodded, then came around to her side and pushed open the door. She walked past him, and her arm brushed his coat.

"Alan . . ." Kay breathed deeply, taking a seat in the armchair in the corner of his office. "I've been doing a lot of thinking. I know"—she laughed—"you're going to tell me I think too much. Well, you're right. But this time, at least, it got me somewhere."

"I'm glad to hear it." He sat on the edge of his desk, his long legs stretched out in front of him, his eyes never leaving her face.

"Look," she said, blushing as she read the intensity in his gaze and thinking that he had never looked more attractive to her—paler and thinner, perhaps, but very solid. "I've been horribly selfish for the past few months, and I want to make it up to you. To us," she added. "I don't know how, exactly, but I guess it'll come to me." She stopped, thinking she sounded silly. When she'd decided to come and talk to him she had been afraid that she wouldn't know how to begin, how to form the simplest phrases, but it was just the opposite. The emotions that she'd suppressed for so long came to the surface now, trying to pour out in a stream.

"You don't have to explain anything to me, you know that," Alan told her warmly. "You're my wife and I care more about you than anything else in the world. I want us to try again—I'm glad you want to try, too."

Kay listened to him with a strange mixture of feelings. On the one hand she had longed to hear those words from Alan. On the other she was still anxious, not yet wanting them to get to the moment and the conversation they'd avoided for so long.

"I think I should start by being honest and telling you I was forced into coming here." She smiled ruefully, getting up to stand beside the miniature solar system that sat on a table near the door. She touched the little planets, making them spin gently.

"Oh? I take it that pushy Erica and pushy Katherine ganged up on you." He laughed, walking over to stand behind her.

"No, not really. I mean, something's happened that I can only talk to you about, no one else." She turned to face him and as their eyes met the old desire flared up in her. It was true, she realized suddenly. She didn't only want to confide in Alan, she wanted *him,* as only a woman can want a man. But she quickly looked away so that she could deal with the issue she'd come to discuss. "Guess what?" she said flatly. "Erica's pregnant."

"She's . . . ? You mean . . . ? Oh, boy, that's something!" Alan threw back his head and laughed, but when he saw Kay's expression he stopped abruptly. "I'm sorry. It isn't funny. It's just . . . well, the conjunction of the planets, as we say in the business. Amazing how one affects the other. Not that you and Erica are as allied as Jupiter and Mars, but still . . ." He let the thought trail off. "Okay," he continued in a softer tone. "Now tell me how you're taking it."

"When she first told me," Kay began, "I was horrified, even a bit accusatory. I wanted to be happy for her even though I couldn't hide the fact that I was shocked. Can you understand that?"

"Sure I can." Alan nodded, taking her hand in his. "I'd probably have had the same reaction myself. It was like she'd told you *you* were pregnant, right?"

"Exactly," Kay said, letting her small hand lie comfortably in his large one. It was so like Alan to read her mind, to think the same thoughts. "But that doesn't make it right for me to act like some grief-stricken idiot. As soon as I'd done it I was ashamed of myself, particularly when I sat and listened to her telling Katherine on the phone. She was so joyful, Alan, and so was Mom. I felt like some big gloomy bird hovering over the proceedings."

"Did you tell her that?" he asked.

"No," she admitted. "Not yet."

"Well," he said, still holding her hands tightly, "I hate to ask such a bourgeois question, but who's the lucky father?"

"His name is Mark Sabia and he's an actor. I met him that night you and I had dinner."

"Oh, the guy who's working in Minnesota." Alan nodded. "She told me about him on the phone when we arranged how to get you over to Le Provençal."

"Oh, that." She was suddenly embarrassed about being the problem case, the one everybody had to walk softly around. "Well, I'm not going to behave like that anymore, I can assure you. And I know what you're going to ask next," she rushed on when he tried to interject a comment. "Yes, they're madly in love and somehow they're going to work things out so they can be together. I didn't get far enough to ask anything as boring as 'Are you getting married?' " She laughed and he joined in.

"Only us old staid folks think about things like marriage and commitment and . . ." He paused for a moment, evaluating her mood. ". . . living happily ever after."

He dropped her hand and took hold of her waist, drawing her to him. She let it happen, leaning against his powerful chest and shutting her eyes. She felt his lips on her cheek; then they traveled slowly up to her forehead as one hand slowly caressed her face and hair.

Kay was overwhelmed with his need for her and she responded passionately, throwing her arms around his neck. Her eyes flew open and she saw herself reflected in the deep pools of his brown eyes. There was that look on his face again—the one he had when he stared up at the heavens.

"Alan—" she began, but his mouth came down forcefully over hers, stopping her speech and all sense of time. Their kiss grew deeper as they explored each other with lips and tongues, drawing strength from their desire. How long they stood that way, wrapped in that close embrace, Kay could never have said. When at last they pulled apart they were breathing hard, their foreheads covered with a thin film of perspiration, as though they had run a mile just to find comfort in each other's arms.

"I'm . . . Oh, Alan." She looked at the tiny scar over his temple, at the high cheekbones and thick curly hair of her husband, and wondered how she had been able to live without this sight for so long.

"Let's get out of here," he suggested, running his hand along the sleeve of her silk blouse and making her body tense with longing for him.

"I've got a lot of work. So do you," she reminded him.

"Kay," he cautioned. "We have a lot of unfinished business. That's more to the point."

"I know, but I want to take this slowly. Please, Alan. How about lunch?" she suggested.

"How about a picnic down by the landing in Sausalito where we always went. I'll get box lunches from Le Soupçon and we can—"

"I remember," she said with a small catch in her voice. "Cold curried chicken, pâté, mushroom salad and champagne."

"That's a tall order, lady." Alan laughed, reaching over to hug her. "But if that's what you want, then that's what you shall have."

"That's what we had that night on the sailboat," she said quietly.

He blinked, his mind flashing back eight years to that special picnic. "I borrowed Tim's boat for the night." He nodded. "You got the food, I picked up the wine and off we went."

Kay pulled away from him and went to the window. "We talked about it for hours, just floating on the waves, remember? I kept saying we should wait to get settled in our jobs and you pointed out that we could only get busier professionally, so we might as well dig in now, do everything at once."

"Did I say that?" He frowned. "Sounds a little immature."

"Oh, no," she protested, turning to face him. "I wanted it too. I was always more cautious than you. Even now," she murmured.

"Especially now. I guess it just shows up when you have problems."

Kay bit her lip and tried to tell herself that she'd known even then how different they were, that she'd appreciated the parts of Alan that contrasted with hers, but she knew it was a lie. Just as she'd realized that night at Le Provençal that he wasn't some extension of her, but another whole person, now she realized that he always had been. The amazing thing, considering their differences, was how close they'd always been.

"I do remember that night," he said when she was silent for a while. "You were so afraid you'd be seasick."

"Well, I'd never done it in a boat before." Kay smiled, the mood easing somewhat between them. "How was I supposed to know?"

"But you weren't. Too busy concentrating on our important moment," he reminisced. "I think we even started picking names right after that first time we made love in the bottom of that boat."

"And then you said we ought to try it again, because the pitch of the waves hadn't been conducive to conception earlier in the evening." Kay burst out laughing.

"But my nautical expertise clearly left something to be desired," Alan quipped.

"That wasn't your fault." She suddenly heard what she'd said, and it startled her. Had she ever thought that it *was* his fault that she couldn't get pregnant? They'd gone to every specialist in town, submitting to tests and more tests. They'd talked about adopting, then nearly lost hope when they discovered how difficult the adoption process was.

But then, at last, seven years after they first decided they wanted a child, Kay got pregnant. She knew at once without waiting for the results of the blood test and ran to Alan's office with the news. They were so deliriously happy that they waltzed around the corridors hugging each other, much to the chagrin of his older, more serious colleagues. And when Kay had an amniocentesis as a precautionary measure, because they'd had so much trouble conceiving, Alan was right by her side. The doctor had asked if they wanted to know the sex of the child, because so many couples preferred it to be a surprise. Kay and Alan, true scientists that they were, wanted to know. "It's a healthy little boy," the doctor said. They named him Sean that very night.

"I know it wasn't my fault, or our fault," Alan cut in quietly. "There's no blame to be placed here, Kay."

Kay felt cold suddenly, as terrible pangs of emptiness shot through her. How she hated that feeling, wanted it to stop, wanted to run away from it. But she couldn't anymore, because she had resolved to stop running away.

Alan was by her side before she could even look

up, and his arms locked around her. When she looked up into his eyes she saw what he had been going through all this time without her. It wasn't very pretty, but she loved him for it.

"Alan, I . . . I don't think I can handle lunch. Have dinner with me tonight?" she asked. He nodded and she broke the contact between them.

"I'll pick you up at your office after work. Hey," he called as she started for the door. "You can stay here for a while if you like. Just to be quiet and think."

"Uh-uh." She raised her head and smiled bravely at him. "Enough hard thinking for one morning. I'll see you later."

She walked out of his office and down the corridor, propelled by a new kind of faith in herself and in Alan. She was coming back. It wouldn't be easy, but eventually she'd make it. Whether they could make it together or not was up to her.

Their dinner, at a tiny hole in the wall in Chinatown, was quiet and unemotional. Alan let her lead, taking the conversation where she would. And she found that she was less distracted than she had been for months. She felt more connected, although it would have been hard to say she felt comfortable. Everything was still an effort, because it was like the first time all over again.

They finished their meal at about ten and wandered outside to the car. "How's the old girl been behaving lately?" Kay asked casually, patting the Subaru's front fender.

"Perfect. Let's give her a spin." He opened the door for her, lightly touching Kay's arm as he helped her in. The pressure of his fingers burned through her light coat, and it was odd, because he'd touched her so many times—even earlier in his office—and she couldn't recall having ever felt that way. She was on fire, about to jump out of her skin.

"Anything wrong?" he asked as he climbed in on his side and started the engine. She was loosening the light scarf around her neck and shrugging off her coat to reveal the low-cut blue silk blouse she'd changed into at the office. She always kept something a little fancy in her closet in case she went out right after work.

"Must be the Chinese food—MSG syndrome." She shrugged. "I'm hot all over."

He reached over her to roll down her window and again she blistered at his accidental touch. But, like someone with a high fever, she was shivering slightly, even though she was unusually warm. Other than those symptoms, however, she felt marvelous, filled with excitement and a sense of being alive that she had once feared she'd lost.

"Are you okay? You never used to react badly to Chinese food," he said in a worried tone.

"I'm terrific." She grinned. "Honest. It'll pass."

"I hope not," Alan whispered. "Just in case it's me and not something you ate."

She blushed and turned from him as he pulled away from the curb, wondering how it could be that a thirty-three-year-old woman felt just like an adolescent on her first date. You went out for a meal and talked politely, then you took a drive someplace, and then . . .

That's how most dates ended up, if both parties were willing, but surely not with a married couple.

Kay was overcome with confusion. One part of her was content just to be with Alan again, but another, deeper part of her craved more, demanded the union of bodies that made them truly one, united against the world.

She was still mulling all this over when she noticed that Alan was driving up Mission Street. Then he turned on his right-turn signal as he headed for the bridge.

"Where are you going?" she asked suspiciously.

"Where do you think?" he countered.

"You're headed for Sausalito—and you weren't going to tell me." She felt panicky all of a sudden. "I can't go there. Not yet, Alan. Please." Tears welled up in her eyes as she spoke.

"Go on, say it, Kay. You don't want to go *home.* But you belong there, with me." He swiftly pulled up beside a fire hydrant and jerked up the emergency brake. Then he reached for her, crushing her in a powerful embrace. His kiss seared her lips, and he would not let her go.

Kay went limp in his arms, submitting as he covered her face and neck with scorching kisses. But when he moved lower, parting her blouse and letting his lips travel down between her breasts, she moaned and clutched at him, urging him not to stop, never to stop. Why had she ever left him? She marveled in a dreamy haze. Why had she insisted that she needed time to make sense of her life? Alan *was* her life. He was the core of her being, the drama, the romance and all the ordinary little things that fit together into a perfect relationship. She'd been blind to think that she could work things out without him. Every day away had only put another barrier between them. Now, suddenly, she wanted to break them all down.

"Alan," she sobbed, her fingers tangled in his hair, "hold me." They kissed again, plumbing the depths of each other's souls. Theirs was the embrace of two people who had long ago learned what gave the other pleasure. And yet there was a new passion starting between them, one that could not be denied.

"Please come home," he begged, his voice ragged with desire for her.

But that was the one thing she couldn't do yet. Shaking her head, she pulled away from him, still not letting go of his hands. "You're going to think I'm nuts," she muttered.

"I always have. I'll take you, nuts or not," he said with a small laugh.

"Really?" She bit her lip and then said, "Let's go to a motel."

"You're kidding."

"I'm perfectly serious." She leaned over to run her tongue along his fingers to the palm of his hand and nipped him lightly, showing him just how serious she was.

His hand caressed her face then, and the look that passed between them was the look of a man and a woman who wanted each other and would not deny their need. "Not a motel." He frowned. "Too tacky. But I do know a place . . ." Reluctantly he moved away from her and restarted the car. There was a determined look on his face as he pulled into traffic.

Twenty minutes later they were in Nihonmachi, San Francisco's Japanese district. Alan took the car down several winding streets decorated with banners and kites. The signs in all the store and restaurant windows were written in Japanese, and several of the buildings were crowned with pagodalike structures.

Soon they reached the hotel that had been his destination. It had a wide entrance, flanked with bonsai trees and flowering chrysanthemums. Alan began to drive through it, but he was stopped by a parking attendant who took the keys and quickly drove the Subaru around to the back of the hotel.

"Where are we?" Kay marveled.

"I've heard about this place. Sounds very exotic. Just right for us." He ushered her through the front entrance and as she passed by she read the placard on the side of the building: "Hotel Sunami."

The lobby was a haven of quiet luxury. A small fountain played in the center, and there were flowers everywhere. Women in traditional Japanese dress hurried past them to the end of the hall, where a shoji screen separated them from the next room. The women knelt, pulled open the screen, and then passed through like shadows.

Kay felt the calm of the place wash over her. Alan was right, of course. A motel, with its starkly modern efficiency, would have been awful—this foreign locale right in the heart of their own city was perfect for clandestine lovers, even married ones. How like Alan to "make a surprise" for her the way he used to. In the early days of their marriage, when they dreamed of their round-the-world tours but couldn't afford two tickets to L.A., Alan would invariably come up with something—

Italian opera on the stereo, a trip to Chinatown, even French croissants served to her in bed by a devastating bearded man wearing a silly beret.

The young desk clerk, who wore Western dress, greeted them with a slight bow, not even glancing around for their nonexistent luggage. "Sir, may I help you?" he asked.

"Yes." Alan smiled, clutching Kay's hand. "We'd like a room, please. Something very luxurious."

"All our rooms are quite excellent." The clerk nodded. "How long a stay will that be, sir?" he asked, handing the register to Alan for his signature.

"We'll start with one night." Alan grinned. With a flourish he wrote, "Mr. and Mrs. Alan Devore."

Kay wanted to laugh, but she was too excited. There was something very special about running off with a man for a night of love, a man you'd thought about and dreamed of for three long months. She and Alan followed the bellhop to their fifth-floor suite, and she gasped with delight as he pulled open the latticed doors and led them inside.

The room was spacious, but simply decorated, the kind of place you could feel at home in, as opposed to the totally interchangeable interiors of most hotel rooms. On one wall was a long terrace that overlooked Post Street and the bay beyond. There was a simple lacquered table in the center of the room, with a black vase filled with cherry blossoms. The wallpaper was a traditional golden-bird print; the two low chairs were upholstered in brocade with a chrysanthemum motif. But Kay couldn't suppress a smile as her eye lighted on the large American-style bed tucked into an alcove and covered with a green brocade spread.

"I don't think I could have managed a tatami mat on the floor," she said after the bellhop had taken his tip and left the room with a bow. "Oh, Alan, this is simply lovely!"

He fixed her with a serious gaze as he came toward her. "*You* are simply lovely."

She felt almost shy as he reached for her hands. Oddly enough, it was hard to remember what this whole process of touching and kissing and caressing was like, because she'd been away from it for so long and it had been out of her consciousness even longer than that. But now she called back the old yearning of the flesh and was titillated by the very thought of lovemaking. No matter what happened between them tonight in this room, she would remember it forever.

Alan drew her close and pressed her against his long, lean body. Her full breasts blossomed when he cupped them and bent over her for a tender kiss. She knew at once that she had recaptured that look of a woman who knows a man's touch. Everything inside her was churning, whirling, like bits of paper caught in a windstorm. She had never wanted anything so much as to sleep with this man at this moment.

But he pulled away and led her across the room, away from the giant bed.

"Alan . . ." she begged, the ache in her growing stronger.

"I think a nice, soothing Japanese bath first," he

said, leading her into the tiled bathroom, which was almost as big as the bedroom. "What about it?" He knelt beside the round blue porcelain tub and turned on the jets. Water spurted from eight different angles and pulsed into the tub with a quiet shushing sound.

He stood up beside her and she could hear his breathing above the sound of the water. "God, how I've missed you," he moaned before reaching up to clasp the back of her head and bring it closer. The long strands of her ash-blond hair fell over his fingers and he sighed, recapturing an experience he'd longed for and dreamed of for months.

Kay trembled at his touch, barely able to stand, although she was leaning against him. She held on to his powerful arms and let him lift her and carry her to the plush white rug on the opposite side of the spacious bathroom.

"I can't wait," he whispered hoarsely as he began to unbutton her silk blouse. It was like the first time for both of them as they feverishly removed each other's clothes. The room was steamy and luxuriantly warm, but neither of them noticed the temperature. They caressed each other intimately as their clothes dropped to the floor, then stood before each other naked, drinking in the sight.

His body looked different to her without clothes on, although of course she had imagined him like this in the privacy of her room at night many times. But seeing him actually before her made the blood rush to her head. She was faint with longing for him.

Alan reached over just for a second to turn off the water, and Kay couldn't contain herself another minute. She draped herself over his broad back, her breasts brushing the fine hairs on his neck. He turned and embraced her fiercely, his mouth coming down on one nipple and teasing it until it obeyed his command and stood up at attention. Only then did he start on the other. Kay thrashed wildly beneath his touch, wanting nothing but the feeling of his hard body on hers.

"Come on." She nearly dragged him out of the bathroom and they collapsed on the bed, rolling over on the elegant spread. Kay moved aside for one second just to push it to the floor, and suddenly Alan was below her, kissing the backs of her knees. She had always been so sensitive there. She gasped and arched back, only to find him waiting and urgent. His eyes never left hers as he continued his pleasure, nibbling gently at her thighs, moving up to her flat stomach and stopping once again at her breasts, which rose to meet him.

He would have continued had Kay not surprised him by locking her legs around his back and pulling him over onto her. "Now," she pleaded.

He entered her with a shudder of delight and she cried out, welcoming him home after such a long journey. There were tears in her eyes, but she wasn't sad, only filled with so much emotion and passion that her own body could not contain it.

"Kay, my darling," he moaned, lifting his weight off her but never breaking their contact. They rocked together then, sensing each other's rhythm and only altering it when their ecstasy carried them further, into realms they had never traveled together.

Kay was conscious of something different between them, a new understanding, a new awareness of what this relationship really meant. But then all thought was suspended as her body's urgency took over, driving her on, whipping her to a frenzy. Alan let it happen, urging her on with quiet words and kisses. It wasn't long, though, before he, too, joined her on that incredible plunge over the brink of normal space and time. They cried out once together, and then Kay cried out a second time while Alan held her, crooning to her softly.

For a long time they lay together, their tangled limbs entwined on the cool sheets, letting their breathing become calmer and quieter. Then Alan rolled to one side of the bed and took a corner of the sheet to wipe her sweating face. "Well," he said, smiling down at her, "I'm afraid our bathwater's cold by now."

"That's the only thing in this whole place that's cold." She grinned.

"MSG syndrome, my foot." He nodded wisely, his beard brushing her forehead as he bent down to kiss it. "Those hot flashes were from pure passion."

"You're right," she agreed happily, snuggling into his arms. Her body felt burnished, totally loved and cared for. "I don't want to go to sleep now," she protested when he leaned over to turn out the lamp on the night table. "Let's talk, Alan."

"Who said anything about sleeping?" he whispered in her ear, biting it gently. "Or talking, for that matter? The night is young, and we have only just begun."

The big three-quarter moon hung above them, watching impassively as the couple embraced once more. And even when the moon vanished at the end of that long night they were still very much awake, and very busy making love.

Chapter Eight

Kay moved very slightly, so as not to wake Alan. He looked so peaceful in sleep, just like a child, without a care in the world. Without even lifting her leg off his, she reached across for his watch which was lying on the night table beside the bed.

Almost five A.M.—she must have been awake for an hour already. There was no use trying to sleep now. Her mind and body were alive with feelings, new and old, and there simply wasn't any way to quiet them enough for her to relax.

She looked at the man beside her and smiled gently. He was so beautiful to her, the person she remembered and yet so much more. He had handled her body with the care and perfection he had always lavished on her. And then, after hours of ardent lovemaking, he had slipped into this blissful dream world. He was calm and still in sleep, just as Sean used to be.

She wrenched her gaze away from Alan's face, trying to blot out the comparison. The morning light was growing stronger now, hitting the golden birds on the wallpaper and making them glint and sparkle. Were the birds cranes? Kay wondered. Or storks, who brought babies? Was it possible that everything in the world would remind her of Sean —that she'd never free herself from those associations? If she could have burned his memory from her mind right then, she would have done it.

The point was, though, that she clung to the memory as a drowning person does to a life preserver. The past was so real to her, and now there was so much else that made it more vibrant— the mild weather, Alan's serene face, the car, the Golden Gate Bridge, the photo of the moon on the door of Alan's office, the planetarium, the nursery at the Academy, and most of all, the night of love she had just spent with her husband. It all made her think of Sean.

He'd been born on a cold February night a week and a half before her due date. She'd been at her desk at home, deeply immersed in a scientific article, and Alan had been busy in the kitchen making eggplant parmigiana. Every once in a while he'd look over at her and notice her massaging her belly or stretching her back.

"This is the stupidest thing I've ever read," Kay complained loudly, tapping the journal angrily with a pencil. "I don't see why they can't— Ow!" she yelped, suddenly clutching her stomach.

"What is it?" Alan was at her side in an instant.

"Baby's just playing soccer with my stomach." She laughed, but her brow was still creased with pain. "Go back to your eggplant."

She then proceeded to read the article aloud to him, adding her pointed editorial commentary whenever she felt that the author had said something particularly dumb. Twenty minutes later she had another contraction.

"I'm going to start timing them," Alan said, turning off the oven.

"Don't be silly. It's weeks away. First babies are never on time."

In response to her nonchalant attitude Alan went to the bedroom for her bag and a fistful of lollipops to keep her "whistle wet" when she started panting during labor. He'd been the one to insist on packing two weeks earlier. As far as Kay was concerned she wasn't going to stop being the compleat scientist and start being a mother until the precise moment of transition arrived.

The contractions started coming every fifteen or twenty minutes on a pretty regular schedule, and after several hours they came closer, first at twelve- and then at ten-minute intervals. Alan picked up the phone to call the hospital, and Kay, still sure that there was no need, asked, "Alan, what *are* you doing?" But then she couldn't protest anymore, because a tidal wave of a contraction gripped her and held her. She fought back the urge to scream.

Alan's face was white as he came to her and began massaging her stomach in slow, round strokes. "Start the breathing, Kay. Come on! Don't fight it. You remember from the course. I'll count for you. Kay, don't give in to the pain. Go with it."

She couldn't even hear his commands, so paralyzed was she by the force storming through her body. But she controlled it despite herself and finally started the breathing. It made her feel powerful, to have conquered the enemy and mastered her own fears.

"Can you make it to the car, sweetheart?" Alan asked at the end of it. "You want me to carry you?"

The pain passed and Kay wiped her forehead, sticking her journal back under her nose. "No, I don't. And you're jumping the gun. Think of the eggplant." She sighed.

"Our son first, eggplant later." Alan settled her in the backseat and drove just under the speed limit across the bridge to the hospital.

Her doctor and several nurses surrounded them as soon as they arrived. She was immediately taken to a comfortable room, where she was examined. Then, with Alan by her side, she continued her breathing. This was more than their baby, she knew. It was the final link in the chain woven between her and Alan. This child would be part of both of them and a separate individual as well, with his own hopes and dreams and fears.

"Concentrate," Alan kept urging her. "Remember the breathing. Let me help you, Kay."

It occurred to her that maybe Alan had paid more attention than she during the natural-childbirth classes. He behaved like an old pro, instructing and encouraging her, supplying her with back rubs, wet washcloths and tender words whenever she looked like she needed them. He talked her through the long eighteen-hour haul. Finally the contractions started coming every two minutes. Alan quickly donned a surgical gown and mask and helped the nurses get her into the delivery room. Then, as if by magic, their child demanded to be born. Sean arrived with the breaking dawn, kicking and squirming, and when the doctor handed him to Kay she was awestruck, not yet able to fathom the amazing and wonderful thing that had just occurred.

" 'Twinkle, twinkle, little star,' " Alan whispered as he lifted Sean in his arms.

"Little star!" Kay had choked out hoarsely, recovering her sense of humor. "He's as big as the whole universe."

But from then on Sean *was* their little star, as bright and perfect as any of the constellations. He was an easy baby, delightful to care for. He rarely cried and almost seemed to understand his parents' devotion to him, their eagerness to make his new life completely happy. At first Alan was a nervous wreck, terrified that he was going to drop the baby or give him a cold or not realize quickly enough what he was asking for when he wailed. Kay was able to reassure him only gradually that Sean wouldn't break.

"Hey," she joked one night, "the kid knows we've never done this before. He'll forgive a few mistakes."

"But how many?" Alan had moaned, not quite sure that he was the model father Kay said he was.

The only thing that had concerned her at that point was that somehow parenthood would change the special relationship that she and Alan possessed. They were such a private, intimate couple, completely wrapped up in each other, as they had been for eight years. Everyone—particularly Katherine—had warned Kay that having a child would turn their life upside down and change it irrevocably.

"You'll see," Katherine had told her when she came for a few days to help out. "It's a different way of life."

Kay listened and said nothing, certain that that wouldn't happen between her and Alan. What they had together was too precious to lose, a new baby notwithstanding. It wasn't only sex, although that was a big part of it. All they had to do was look at each other and the electrical current started pulsing between them. Before the six-week recuperation period was over, they felt it, as strong as ever.

"I can't yet," Kay told Alan softly. "But I want you."

"No reason we have to do it the conventional way." He smiled, nuzzling her right ear. "You just leave it to me."

And then he had shown her the extent of his imagination, exciting her in ways she had never thought of before, exploring new techniques of expressing his love. Their passion was so deep, so vast, that lovemaking could be anything at all, from feathery circles of his fingers around her swollen, full breasts to an infinity of kisses and licks and sweet caresses. There was no need to tell Katherine that she had been mistaken about the baby changing their relationship—her mother could see that very well for herself.

Sean expanded Kay's world; he didn't restrict it.

Oh, it was difficult going back to work that first day after her ten-week maternity leave was over, but the Academy's nursery made even that trauma easier. Alan, Sean and Kay would drive to work together each morning, at which point Maggie Tolan would take over. Sean was the youngest in the nursery, but the others fussed over him and made him at home in their little family. At lunchtime Kay and Alan would take their son for a stroll around the promenade in his carriage, and it wasn't long before he became the most popular person in the California Academy of Sciences. Sean's sunny smile and happy gurgles caused biologists and astronomers alike to comment that the Devores had been blessed with an unusual child.

At first their son was most captivated by the fish at the Steinhardt Aquarium. Kay and Alan would pick him up in front of one of the big tanks and he would fix his tiny hands on the glass, his sharp eyes traveling back and forth with the fish. It almost looked like Sean was watching their movements with professional appreciation.

"I guess he's his mother's child," Alan sighed in mock desperation one day. "Or else he wants to grow up to be Jacques Cousteau."

But at four months all that changed. The Sky Show at the planetarium was clearly Sean's favorite activity from that time on. Kay loved to watch his deep blue eyes taking in the clusters of stars above him, his little fingers reaching higher to pluck one of them down. He never failed to coo with joy at the big heavy moon hanging barely beyond his grasp. He could make the simplest afternoon into an exciting exploration of the unknown, and Kay and Alan often commented that they learned a lot from him. He could make them both see their worlds through his new eyes, his growing mind, his—

"Kay! What is it?" Alan raised himself on one elbow and cupped the other arm around her. "What's wrong?"

Kay hadn't even realized until he touched her that she was crying. "Nothing," she whispered blankly. What was it? What had she seen there, in the back of her mind? It was gone now.

"Honey, it's over," Alan crooned, taking her in his arms. "You were thinking about Sean. I can tell."

"No!" she denied, somehow unable to share this with him, even after their night of passion.

"Why do you have to lie to me, Kay?" Alan asked, his brown eyes so deep with feeling that she could have drowned in them. She looked away from his intense gaze.

"Listen to me!" he yelled, grabbing her wrists to get her attention back. "I've stood about all I can take. You act as if this were your own private tragedy. You hoard all the pain for yourself so you can be the big martyr. Go ahead, admit it," he challenged. "If you crowd me out there's all the more pain for you, right?" He refused to go easy on her, not after the closeness they'd attained the night before. He couldn't risk losing her again.

Kay was shivering, but her naked body wasn't nearly as exposed as her raw emotions. Even as she jerked out of his powerful embrace she knew that she was making a terrible mistake, maybe the worst of her life. "I have to get out of here," she whispered, reaching for her clothes.

He pulled the blouse out of her hand and stood towering over her, his muscular form more imposing than she'd ever seen it. "Sean was my son, too," he growled, holding her in an iron grip. "You make it seem like you're the only one allowed to grieve. Stop being so damn greedy, Kay."

"What do you mean, 'greedy'?" she exploded.

"You cling to his memory like a miser," Alan thundered, snatching her hands and pinning them in back of her. "You keep all the pain to yourself. What for? Are you trying to show the world that you loved him more than anyone else—is that it? Are you trying to show me that you loved him more than I did?"

The bluntness of Alan's words was like a bludgeon beating Kay down. She tried to get free of him, to shut him out once again. But to her amazement he suddenly dropped her hands and walked away from her. He stood silhouetted against the window, his broad shoulders slumped.

"I meant every word I ever said to you. I meant it when I asked you to marry me, when I said I wanted us to have a child, when I told you I believed times would be good for us again. And I mean it now when I say I'm not going to sit on the edge of my seat for the rest of my life waiting for you to face up to reality."

Kay couldn't move, too stunned by his words to think about herself. "What are you saying?" she breathed.

He faced her, his eyes hard and unyielding, the

lines etched deeply around his mouth. "I care about you," he said quietly. "I always will. I'm determined to be with you, but it can't just be on your terms. You can avoid the issue, live under your damn cloud, do whatever you want. I'll be here for a while and I'll stick by you until you come to your senses—as long as I know that you really want me. You've never told me what I'm supposed to do to make things easier for you, so I'm telling you what *I* want from my wife. Do you understand me?"

Kay's head rocked with what he'd just told her. "I think so," she murmured. "You mean that if I won't start over with you, *you'll* start over with someone else."

He sighed, a long, drawn-out moan of anguish. "Oh, God, that was the last thing on my mind. I'm saying I can't wait forever. It hurts too much to be disappointed by everyone I care for. Does this make sense to you?"

She didn't answer, simply gazed into his strong face, memorizing every part of it as though she might never see it again. "We have to go to work," she said meekly.

"That's right." He nodded sardonically, stalking over to the bathroom. "Change into your safe, scientific personality. Make it all clinical and removed from yourself, analyze the night we just spent together into its component parts."

"If you'd just stop accusing me!" she burst out. "That makes it so much worse."

"Does it?" he asked quietly. "Seems to me you do a far better job on yourself than I ever could." He turned away and she heard the sound of the water running in the sink. "I'll be through in here soon. Then I'll drive you to work."

"Don't bother," she called. "I'll take the—"

He appeared at the door, his naked body nearly filling the frame. "I said I'll drive you," he countered hotly. "Even if you aren't ready to be my wife again, even if you never are, I want you to know that I never stopped being your husband. And even if it's a rotten pretense, we're going to walk into that Academy together, so help me God."

His tone brooked no objection. She waited for him on the edge of the bed, fingering the soft cotton sheet. All of her defenses were gone, obliterated by his words. How could she be logical and sensible in the face of his threat? Either she came around and figured out what she wanted, or he wouldn't be there when she was ready for him. And the hard truth had suddenly penetrated, shocking her with its simplicity: What she had thought of for so long as her problem was really theirs.

The day dragged by, and it was nearly impossible for Kay to concentrate on work. She dropped a trayful of instruments all over the floor and couldn't for the life of her remember whether she had or hadn't unpacked the cartons of nutrients that had come in the previous day.

What was worse was that she'd committed herself to go to Erica's dance class that afternoon. All she wanted to do now was go over to Alan's office so they could work things out, but she had no way to get in touch with Erica, who was working as a movie extra on location. No, there was nothing to do at five-thirty but grab her purse and exercise clothing and go to the address Erica had scribbled on an index card for her.

She arrived at the studio a little late, and climbed the rickety stairs to the dressing room, a cheery hole in the wall that smelled of sweat and energy. Erica was already there in her leotard and tights.

"There you are! Donny hates people being late, so move it, sis."

"Okay; all right." Kay shrugged, quickly stripping off her clothes. She couldn't help but think of that morning, when she'd put those clothes on. The image of Alan's naked body swam before her eyes.

"Say, you've lost weight," Erica murmured, sitting down beside her. "I hadn't noticed before." She patted her own stomach and looked in the mirror. "You think they make maternity leotards?"

"I bet they make maternity toe shoes, for heaven's sake." Kay gave her sister a playful push as the bell rang, indicating the end of the last class and the beginning of theirs.

"Now, I warn you," Erica said as they took their places on the big green mats that covered the studio's clean pine floor, "Donny's a taskmaster. He's always awful to newcomers. Just watch me and don't quit in the middle of an exercise."

"I'm surprised at you," Kay whispered as the teacher strode into the room and snapped on his cassette recorder, which blared an upbeat rendition of an old pop tune. "I never quit *anything.*"

And in fact, as the class progressed and Kay really threw herself into it, she found herself feeling more confident, completely in tune with her body. Could it have been one night of love that did it for her? She glanced at herself in one of the mirrors that lined the far wall and saw herself just as she was—a petite woman with ash-blond hair and a trim figure, wearing a red-and-gray-striped leotard that fit much more smoothly than the last time she'd worn it, just after she'd given birth and was determined to get back into shape as fast as she could. Now the stretchy fabric molded itself easily to her slim form, as did the matching tights.

"That is great, ladies," Donny, the instructor, announced. "But that was the easy part. Now I want you to work!"

There was a chorus of groans, but Kay felt like she was flying. There was virtually nothing she couldn't do now. Even her argument with Alan had been part of her new energy, the rhythmic excitement that pulsed through her and vibrated out to her very nerve endings. Somehow the feeling brought her back to the night before, to Alan's body heavy on hers, his lips driving her to the limits of desire and then pushing her over the edge. A night in his arms made her safe and secure, but, more than that, it canceled out the worry that perhaps she had waited too long before going back to him. As she moved across the floor she made a firm resolve: There would be no more silence between them—ever.

"That's it! Who *are* you, anyway?" Donny came up behind her just as she'd finished a complicated set of steps.

"I'm Kay," she panted, wiping drops of moisture from her forehead.

"Well, listen, Kay, I don't know where you got

all this energy, but it's catching. Everyone, watch Kay. She takes to this dance class like a duck to water. Let's have it, now, ladies. Work off that steam! Get rid of those inner demons. *Exorcise,* don't exercise!" Donny quipped.

Half an hour later, when the class was finally over, Kay and Erica walked back into the dressing room together. Erica clapped her sister on the back. "I don't know what got into you. Or him! He never praises anyone. Guess you're just a natural." She sighed.

Kay laughed happily and sat down to mop her wet hair with a towel. There was nothing to it when you felt good about yourself. You could do anything.

Even go home, Kay realized. And that was exactly where she was going. Back to Sausalito.

Chapter Nine

The streets felt just the same, only colder than when she'd last been there. There was the leather shop where she'd once bought Alan a vest; there was the bookstore with its tiny café upstairs where you could sit and read and drink coffee all day, if you wanted.

The bus had deposited her on Bridgeway, right off the water, and she began to stroll, getting the feel and smell of Sausalito back into her mind and heart. The steep hills dotted with little white houses smiled down at the army of masts lining the dock, and beyond the bridge San Francisco gleamed in the distance.

Kay turned right on Princess Street and walked past the jewelry store where she and Alan had bought their wedding bands. She kept going, past the shopping district, up the hill toward the residential section. Her heart pounded around in her chest as she approached Winthrop, the street she'd lived on for four happy years.

They'd bought their house, with a little help from Kay's parents and from Alan's father, Jack, before they were really able to afford it. It was a perfect house, a two-story white stucco with a front porch and a back deck that afforded a lovely view of the bay. They'd worked so hard to get it just the way they wanted it, picking up antiques here and there whenever they found something they liked. It wasn't large by any standards, but it was very comfortable. Just thinking about it made Kay feel warm, at home.

There it was! Tucked around a bend in the steep street, surrounded by a few nice trees and some scrubby bushes Kay had been meaning to pull out for years. *Their* house. It was just one of hundreds; it didn't stand out in any particular way, yet it had been special to two people. Kay palmed the key in her sweaty hand and stood there staring at the house.

For two days now Alan's words had sounded in her brain: "I never stopped being your husband," he'd said. She asked herself if she truthfully could say that she'd never stopped being his wife. Well, it was hard to answer that one. Oh, she'd been faithful, of course, there was no question about that, but there was more to it than physical and emotional allegiance. It was true that she'd never stopped loving Alan, but she'd shut him out when she closed herself into that private world of hers. There was no reason for it, not anymore, and she intended to tell him and show him just how much she cared. She would make up for their lost time somehow.

She approached the front porch tentatively. The reason she'd come that day was that Alan had mentioned over dinner that night before they went to the hotel that he was going to a conference in Palo Alto. She'd taken off early from the lab, not even telling Ada where she was going. She felt like a real sneak thief, dressed in her trench coat with a fedora hat pulled down over her brow. But she had to do this her way, at her own pace.

Boy, if the neighbors see me, she thought with a sudden laugh, they'll probably call the police. "Hey, lady," the officer would demand, "what are you hanging around here for?"

"Well, you see, officer," Kay would answer, "I'm trying to pick up the pieces of my life. I want to come back here to my little house and live with the man I adore."

She smiled ruefully to herself and took a step closer to the porch. It needed painting, she noticed. Even so, it looked great. The key was heavy in her hand and she turned it over and over, debating with herself. She'd always had this house key with her, and when she was in Golden she'd taken it out occasionally, just to make some contact with her old life. What would happen now if she used this key and walked inside? Would all the dozens of little familiar sights and smells and associations be more than she could handle?

"Well, Kay," she said aloud, taking the porch stairs two at a time, "you'll never know till you try."

The key slipped into the lock easily; it belonged

there. And I do too, she thought, swinging the door open. Before she could focus on anything, the smell of the house embraced her, that familiar indescribable scent that was partly Alan, partly her and mostly the house itself. She shut her eyes and breathed deeply of it, the subtle aroma overwhelming her like the bouquet of a fine wine. Yes, this was home. She couldn't deny that there was an important piece of her here, and a very happy one, at that. There were fond memories in this house, not just frightening ones, and those good memories were what she had come to recapture.

The quiet was strange. Alan loved music, and he always had something playing on the stereo—a Beethoven string quartet or some Renaissance madrigals. The house without music seemed like a museum after hours.

She walked slowly from the foyer to the living room. It was just as she'd left it months ago, and yet, seeing it now, the colors seemed brighter and newer, as if the whole place had been covered with a veil that had suddenly been lifted off for her inspection. The blue-and-rust Oriental rug that Alan's grandmother had given them from her own den was like an old friend to Kay, as were the straw masks on the wall that she and Alan had bought in Mexico on their honeymoon.

Kay stared at the line of bookshelves, the familiar titles just where she knew they'd be. She could still tell the books she'd read from the ones Alan had read—their taste in current fiction and nonfiction wasn't always identical—and she could even remember when and where the books had been purchased. They were all mixed in together, his and hers, arranged in some amazingly logical way without regard to topic or author or whose book it was. It was a joke between them that since they both had photographic memories they didn't need a filing system.

It was the same with the row of albums stored in the cabinets by the front bay windows. Alan's classical records shared the space with Kay's folk and country selections. Kay ran her hand along the edge of the cabinet, looking at the physical proof of how intertwined their lives really were.

She walked behind the couch and over to the mantel, where they kept figurines and photographs. There was one of Alan at age six, playing ball with his father, and one of her at her high-school graduation. She'd always loathed that picture, but because Alan was nuts about it, it remained on the mantel. There was their formal wedding shot, both of them looking nervous and slightly uncomfortable in their period clothes, and one taken by Erica at the very end of their wedding day when everyone else had gone home. The photo showed Kay and Alan leaning together comfortably, pulling off their shoes in great relief. Beside all of these was a picture of Sean at three months.

Kay picked up that last picture in its tiny frame, engraved around the side with her baby's date and time of birth, and his weight, seven pounds, three ounces. He looked very calm in that shot, like a little Buddha, his big eyes shining as he gazed sedately out at the camera. "This picture clearly shows he has genius potential," Alan had said when they put it up on the mantel. "No," Kay had countered, "it shows he just woke up from a nap and he's still zonked."

She put the picture back in place and moved around the room. Gingerly she touched the back of the big brown velvet armchair where Alan liked to curl up with a good book. Running her fingers along the plush material reminded her of how she used to come up behind him and run her fingers through his curly hair, teasing him until he put the book down and paid attention to her. Once they'd made love in that armchair, she recalled with a smile. He'd pulled her down over him and kissed her longingly, at the same time easing her skirt up over her hips. When she could no longer stand the maddening touch of his hands, she'd straddled the chair, her legs flopping over the arms, and they'd joined together quickly and fiercely, needing the sustenance that only their two bodies as one could give.

She made a circle around the chair and her eye suddenly caught an unfamiliar sight. That lamp on the end table—she'd never seen it before. It made her anxious just thinking about the fact that Alan had bought something on his own while she was away. He'd always claimed to have lousy taste, not to know what went with what, although naturally that wasn't true. But he'd purchased something for their house without even thinking about her, and it filled her with an unaccountable sense of jealousy to realize that she wasn't indispensable. It was a nice lamp, a simple blue ginger jar with a cracked glaze. It went with everything—and with the life Alan had had without her for several months now.

She told herself that she was being silly to wonder if someone, a woman perhaps, had helped him pick it out. Actually it was worse to think of him choosing it himself, because of what that implied. And once again it reminded her that the time for procrastinating had run out.

She sighed and walked toward the door that led to the kitchen. She had to see it all, the whole house, had to make it hers again. Only then would she know she belonged. Just as she put her hand on the door, the calm was suddenly shattered by the ring of the telephone.

Kay's eyes shot open, her heart pounding. For a split second she wanted to bolt, to run out the door and down the block before someone caught her. "Oh, don't be ridiculous," she said aloud. "No one knows you're here. And suppose they did? So what?"

She stared at the phone, debating with herself. One of Alan's colleagues? No, they'd be at the conference with him. His father? But why would he call in the middle of the day? It couldn't be another woman, could it? Now, that was absurd—the dumbest thought she'd had in weeks. He'd said that there was no one else.

For some reason she couldn't stand not knowing. And part of her wanted it to be Alan, as silly as that sounded. There was no sense in his calling his own house, and yet she still hoped. On the sixth ring, feeling weird and panicky, she lifted the receiver.

"Hello?" She sounded breathy, as though she'd run a mile.

"Hello, Kay? Is that you?"

She had the strangest feeling, holding that phone. The man on the other end wasn't Alan, but he knew who she was, had known she'd be there. The voice was familiar, but she couldn't place it.

"Hello, Kay?" he repeated. "Are you still there?"

"Yes . . ."

"Kay, it's me, Johnny. Johnny Pallas. Boy, am I glad I found you!" he said jubilantly.

Kay's heart sank, and she felt oddly lost in the familiar room as she made contact with the voice. Johnny, from Golden. But how had he found her? And why now, just when her life was about to straighten out?

"Johnny! I . . . How in the world did you get this number?" she asked in a numb haze.

He laughed, a hearty, open sound that reverberated over the phone wires. She could almost imagine him tucking his hair behind his ears and crossing his beanpole legs in front of him. "My God, I've been going crazy trying to locate you, Kay. Your mother wouldn't give me a clue, and believe me, I tried. I've been over there every day, practically, pleading my case, but that woman has a heart of stone. Well, then, just by chance, a couple of days ago she mentioned your sister Erica and I remembered that you had told me she lived in San Francisco. So I called directory assistance and got her number. Hey, Kay, how *are* you?" he asked in a caring tone. "I miss you something awful."

Kay sat heavily on the arm of the sofa. "You mean Erica gave you this number?"

"Are you kidding? I don't know what it is with your family, Kay, but she's as bad as your mother.

She said she had no idea who I was and she wasn't in the habit of giving out a married woman's phone number to a strange man who claimed to know her, so I should just forget it. She told me to leave you alone, or else. But I figured I had to talk to you directly and not just sit back and let your relatives tell me how you felt, you know? Well, you said you lived in Sausalito, so I figured maybe you went back there. I got the numbers for every single Devore in town. This is the fifth one I've tried." He laughed. "But, Kay, it's worth it just to hear your voice again. Well, talk to me, woman—say something. Aren't you glad to hear from me?"

"Surprised, I'll say that. Johnny, I don't really—"

"Now, you listen to me. I'm not going to believe a fool thing your sister and mother tell me. I've thought this over real carefully for weeks now, debating with myself whether I should call you or not. After all, I respect the institution of marriage. I think that once you've taken that vow, you better think long and hard before you break it. And it's taken this long for my real feelings to surface. Kay, I don't want to hear about your husband—I know something can be done about that because if there's a will, there's a way. I called for one reason, all right? I've never said this before, to anybody—"

"Johnny, please!" She knew what he was about to say, and it wasn't what she wanted to hear.

"Kay, I love you and I want you to be my wife. We'll work everything out in due time, but I just have to know how you feel."

She sighed and loosened her grip on the receiver. Why was everything so complicated? She couldn't deal with this right now. "Johnny, I told you when I left Golden that I was your friend. That's how I feel now—that's *all* I feel." It hurt her to hurt him, but she had to be honest with him. She owed him that.

"Look, I know this is abrupt, and I can't deny that our relationship wasn't the big passionate thing they write about in books. But, Kay, since you've been gone I've realized how much you mean to me. I care deeply about you. The time we spent together was precious to me—we didn't need sex or commitment or anything. I saw you were hurting over the breakup of your marriage, so it was hard to get as close as I wanted. But now, well, I think we could be a lot more than good friends. I think, given half a chance, we could be lovers, partners, everything. I'm in love with you."

Kay ached for him. He was so earnest and sincere, but he'd clearly made up something between them that had never existed. Again she thought of Alan's words: "I've never stopped being your husband." Now, as she listened to Johnny's pleas, she knew that she had never stopped being Alan's wife. He was the only man in the world whose words of love and acts of tenderness meant anything at all to her.

"Johnny," she said, "I can't let you go on like this. It's not fair to you."

"Hear me out, Kay," he begged, his voice cracking. "I plan to give you all the time you want to heal. I'm willing to wait for you to get over the life you had before, honest. I didn't really know how bad I needed you until you left Golden, but I do now."

"But *I* don't feel that way," Kay protested.

"Look, I never told you the whole story. I think it's important that you know."

"You don't have to say a thing," he interrupted. "I could see the story written on your beautiful face. The pain was all there, behind your eyes—I saw it the moment I met you. And if you stay with him now it'll be worse, Kay. I guarantee that. But I can make it better."

"It's not him, Johnny. There's more to it than that."

"I don't want to hear about him, I told you," Johnny cut in angrily. "You know in your heart that I'm the one who really loves you and understands you. Come back to Colorado, Kay. Come back to me."

She shook her head sadly. "No, Johnny. I'm staying with Alan, with my husband." Saying the words strengthened her will to return to Alan for good. Now she was sure that this was the right thing, the only thing, to do.

"I refuse to accept that," he countered stubbornly. "Kay, I want you to take some time and consider my proposal. Think of yourself for a change—not what your mother or sister wants, or what *he's* asking for. Just you. I'm going to make you happy, Kay, and get rid of all that sadness your husband saddled you with in the past. I swear to it! You think about that, and give me a call and we'll talk some more. Now, listen, I'm warning you, if I don't hear from you soon I'm coming out to California to get you."

"You can't do that," she said sharply.

"I can and I will. Think about it, Kay. I'm serious."

Johnny hung up and Kay sat there holding the receiver. She could still hear the emotion in his voice coming through to her. What a terrible mess, she thought as she placed the receiver in its cradle. How totally blind she'd been, oblivious of someone else's feelings because she was so tied up in her own. Johnny had fallen head over heels for her, but she'd never noticed.

She got up, left the living room and wandered down the corridor that led to the three bedrooms. How could Johnny ever understand? She'd never really told him anything about Alan. He'd just assumed that Kay had fallen out of love with her husband. And he'd never known anything at all about Sean.

She walked past the master bedroom, purposely averting her eyes so that she could concentrate on the one memory she agonized over, the one she'd shut out for so long. The guest bedroom on the other side of the hallway didn't even attract her sidelong glance. Where she had to go was the small room at the end of the hall. The nursery.

The door was ajar and she pushed it open, making her hand work against her will. They had moved the crib and the chest of toys to the basement, where they wouldn't see them, but the rest of the furniture—the rocker, the bureau and the long counter that had been used as a changing table—was still in place. Alan had stayed up all one night painting the walls a sunny lemon color and the trim a glossy white, because they both hated the idea of pink for girls and blue for boys. The color did nothing to cheer Kay up now, though. She had been dreading her visit to this room for months. How could Johnny possibly ever fathom that?

She sat in the rocker, pulling her trench coat around her. Sunlight streamed through the window and glinted off the mobile of multicolored clouds that hung from the ceiling. Kay had sat here so many times in the past, holding Sean and nursing him, while Alan watched or got everything ready for changing him. The perfect little family picture —mother, father and son. Until that awful night.

They'd had a wonderful evening. It was a mild July night, cool enough for them to use the barbecue on the back deck. Alan did the cooking because he said that women were incapable of making a steak taste properly charred when they cooked outside. Men had a natural gift, but it was not scientifically provable. Kay didn't mind, because that left her free to play with Sean, who was completely fascinated with a new toy that Lena had brought over. Sean, at five months, had an astonishing range of sounds and facial expressions. His attention span was much longer than that of most babies his age, and he dealt with his new toy as carefully as his father dealt with the steaks.

"Don't you think he's beginning to look like me?" Alan pondered as he prepared the coals. "Right around the mouth, see?"

"No, not really. His smile is much more like Katherine," Kay objected. She picked up her son and cuddled him against her shoulder. He gave a gigantic burp. "Okay, fella, bedtime—for a while, anyway. Maybe he'll sleep through the night tonight and I can have you all to myself." She smiled suggestively at her husband.

"Now, that would definitely be the mark of an intelligent and compassionate baby," Alan declared, coming over to kiss his wife and then his son.

It was about eight-thirty when Sean finally fell asleep in his crib and Kay came out with a bottle of wine to join Alan on the deck. Their steaks were done, so they started on dinner. Kay served the salad while Alan sliced the meat into delectable slivers, one of which he fed her with his fingers.

"Yummy," she declared.

"So are you," he said.

They lingered over that meal, the starlight and one candle illuminating them. They talked about hundreds of things, about their careers and office gossip and what Sean might do when he grew up.

"Probably stay as far away from science as he can get. Be one of those humanists, you know," Alan grumbled.

"Or a businessman. He might just take after your father."

"I don't think so. He's got that dreamy look in his eyes—probably wants to be a newspaperman or conduct an orchestra. After all, he hears music all the time—I keep some Bach or Mozart going so he'll get to like it."

Kay laughed. "With your luck he'll be a rock musician."

"Oh, no!" Alan wailed. "As long as he doesn't want to live on a space station or the moon or whatever's popular at the turn of the next century. It'd be too long between visits."

They held hands over the table and shared one of those wonderful moments they'd had so many of since the birth of their son. They could see his whole life unfolding before them, even though the specifics were missing. He'd go to school, make friends, probably skin his knees a lot playing hard, join some ball team, outgrow his clothes, and suddenly he'd be a teenager. And then would come the girlfriends and maybe a car and college applications.

"Pretty soon," Alan said, "he'll be right where we are now. A little house and a career to worry about, then a family."

"God, we'll be so old then," Kay complained. "I'll have wrinkles and midriff bulge and you'll be terribly distinguished-looking—bald, but with a fantastic white beard."

"Don't you believe it!" Alan shook his fist in mock threat. "We'll still be gorgeous. You will, anyway."

"Well, I can only try." Kay shrugged modestly. But then the joking stopped as he took her in his arms and pressed his body tightly against hers.

"You drive me wild, you know that?" he whispered. "You always will." They kissed with an intensity of feeling that sent shivers through both of them. "Leave the dishes," Alan said, taking her by the hand. "I'll do them later."

It was understood—they wanted each other. They no longer needed any words to convey that enormous push toward one another that invariably ended in bed, their naked bodies lying side by side. Their love was so strong that they needed nothing but the slight impetus of a look, a sigh, a shared thought, to drive them together. It was a force larger than they could describe, so they didn't try to, simply let it have its way.

"You go on," Kay murmured, pulling the sliding door to the deck shut behind them. "I'll just check on Sean."

"Want me to do it?" Alan offered.

"You take the early-morning shift." She kissed his nose. "Right now, just go wait for me."

"Don't be long."

She tiptoed down the hall to the baby's room, flicking off the lights as she went. Opening Sean's door, she peeked in. The room was calm and quiet, lit only by the night-light on the far wall. Kay loved this room—she and Alan hadn't done much to it and yet it felt secure and warm, as though it knew it had its own responsibility to protect their son. Good things seemed to emanate from the very walls.

She walked in softly, glancing down at her baby. He was lying on his stomach, his head turned to the left and his right leg half-bent in perfect imitation of his father asleep. Kay debated with herself about waking him—he was so peaceful—but decided to check his diaper anyway.

You're so thorough, so practical, she commented to herself as she put her hand on his wet bottom. Won't even let the poor little fellow get an hour's sleep.

"C'mon, you, let's change this thing. I promise not to wake you up too much." Lifting Sean, Kay sensed something. Something was different—what was it? Suddenly she was terribly frightened, though she had no idea why. Through his sleep sack she felt how cold he was. Too cold. In the dark she could see that Sean's eyes were wide open, staring.

"God!" she breathed. "Oh, please, God!" Carrying her precious burden, she raced to the light switch on the far wall and turned it on. Sean's skin was an unearthly color, his lips blue and pallid.

"*No!*" she screamed. "Alan! My God!"

The only thing she could think of was that he had swallowed something or stifled himself with his pillow. She clutched him close, murmuring soundless words as she pressed her mouth to his tiny one. Slowly . . . one, two in . . . one, two out. Alan came dashing in the door before she could get a second breath.

"What is it?" He looked puzzled at first, then panic-stricken when he saw her with the baby curled into her body like an animal protecting its young.

She didn't answer but kept up the breathing, mindlessly trying to pump air from her lungs into Sean's.

"For God's sake, Kay, let me see him!" Alan demanded.

When she handed the baby to her husband they both gasped at the sight of him. This jolly, happy infant, always gurgling or playing or smiling, was as still as death.

Then Kay was sobbing without tears, reaching for him as Alan felt for a pulse, rocking and shaking him. When he got no response he tried mouth-to-mouth resuscitation again, yelling at Kay to count for him, to keep up the rhythm. But she could do nothing except blink in silent horror.

"Get on that phone, call the pediatrician. Where's Dr. Teller's number, Kay?" Alan asked firmly.

"In my book. Oh, Alan! He's—"

"Call him!"

The doctor told them to meet him at the hospital after asking a few questions. He also told them not to be optimistic.

"But he was always fine before this, doctor," Kay cried into the phone. "He never had colic, never even had sniffles. He's the healthiest baby! But he's not breathing."

The doctor's silence told her more than she needed to know. Without even a good-bye she hung up and raced downstairs to join Alan. They drove over the bridge at breakneck speed, Kay holding their child in her lap. The worst of it was that she was a scientist. She knew what the human body could take and how long it could go without oxygen. She didn't need a doctor to tell her that Sean was dead.

Sanford Teller, a thin man in his late fifties with a kind smile and a no-nonsense manner, was waiting for them at the emergency entrance. He took the baby from Kay and shook his head. "I'm terribly sorry," he said softly.

His assistant took the still, small body and began walking swiftly down the corridor.

"Where are you going?" Kay screamed, running after him. "That's my baby!"

The young man turned and looked at Dr. Teller, who motioned him to go on as he took Kay firmly by the shoulders and marched her toward his consultation room. Alan followed slowly behind them, his eyes fixed and staring.

"You can't look back now, Kay," the doctor told her. "It's all over."

He led the Devores inside his office. They sat together on the couch, inches apart but not touching, the two of them in such deep shock that they were scarcely aware of it when the doctor closed the door behind them. His face was grim when he took a seat behind his desk.

"I don't have to tell you that the worst has happened," he began. "You knew that long before you got here."

"What was it?" Alan demanded, his voice a hoarse rasp of pain. "What killed him?"

"It's a rare occurrence known as SIDS—sudden-infant-death syndrome. You've probably heard it called crib death. Happens very rarely—maybe two per thousand babies in the United States die of it each year. It kills quickly and painlessly and the horror of it is that it kills only the healthy babies, like Sean."

"What did I do?" Kay moaned, dropping her head into her hands. She felt guilt for everything and blamed herself. The times she hadn't changed him quickly enough, the times when he cried and she didn't know why, leaving him in the day-care center so that she could have a career—it was all her fault. She didn't even think of Alan, sitting beside her with tears on his handsome face and an uncomprehending look in his eyes.

"It's nothing you did or didn't do, Dr. Devore," the doctor assured her. "Medical science can do a lot these days with illnesses we understand. But crib death is a mystery, with lots of shadowy clues leading nowhere. We know that many babies, many adults, for that matter, stop breathing for intervals of several seconds during sleep. That's a condition called apnea. And it's quite normal, depending on the length of time of each interval, of course. Certain babies may regularly have a hiatus of ten to fifteen seconds between breaths and nothing ever happens to them. Unless you sat by the crib all night, every night, and listened, you'd never be aware of their apnea.

"But it's the babies who go beyond fifteen seconds whom we have to worry about, because they become the victims of crib death. These children are usually from two to four months old, very healthy, except that some may have a slight cold before it happens. Usually the syndrome occurs in winter, but not always—here we are in July. Sometimes the mother was a heavy smoker during the pregnancy—but you tell me you haven't touched a cigarette since you were a teenager. The answer to your question, therefore, is a big riddle."

"I don't know what to do now," Kay murmured. "I feel so lost." Alan put his arm around her and she scarcely felt it.

"You will be lost for a while," the doctor counseled. "The best thing to do is cry, get it out, mourn together. But don't blame yourselves. Your child is dead, but you have a life ahead of you both. And if you decide at some point in the future to have another baby, there are things we can do to help."

That was it. The last straw. How could this man

be so unfeeling as to suggest another child? Kay thought. There would never be anyone to replace Sean, ever. When she walked out of that hospital she silently closed the door on the possibility of having a family. That part of her life was over.

She didn't cry after that in front of Alan. Their parents came to the funeral, and she simply coped, going through the ritual like a robot. Alan kept wanting to talk about it, to go over it again, but she couldn't bear that. The silence grew between them like a weed, winding itself around her heart and squeezing out all emotion. She felt as dead as her infant son.

Alan did everything he could to help them pick up their lives again, but it was impossible. Everything they did, from driving to work in the morning to looking out the window at the stars at night, reminded them of Sean. The problem was that their ways of grieving were so different. Alan wanted to explore every emotion; he wanted to talk about Sean. He looked up at the stars and moon and shook his head in sad wonder. "Sean is out there somewhere," he'd say, "even though he can't come home." Other days, when he couldn't get through to Kay at all, he'd yell and rant, his rage at her mingling with his fury at Sean's death.

Kay, on the other hand, busied herself with tiny details and raced around in circles, meanwhile becoming enormously self-critical. She knew it had to be her fault. She wasn't meant to be a mother, that was clear. She would never have another child, she told herself, but she longed for the touch of Sean's tiny hands, the feel and scent of his baby skin. As for Alan, she hated his insistence on bringing everything out into the open. For a while she even thought that she hated him and his moods, his anger and his grief. Except, of course, that she didn't hate him at all. He was the only person she could turn to, if she chose to.

Her confused emotions and thoughts doubled back on each other and made her doubt her own competence as a woman, as a person. She would try to talk about her feelings with Dr. Teller and Alan—really try—and then suddenly not be able to remember when she'd last had a legitimate feeling. She'd retreat to her office and work herself silly, forgetting about meals and sleep. Her world had fallen apart.

After three months of this Kay saw another difference between her and Alan. He'd made his peace with death, and he'd done it just the way the doctor and the books counseled: He'd shared his grief with his parents and close friends; he'd talked it out and accepted it at last. She, on the other hand, had done it all wrong, bottling it up, avoiding it, denying it. She'd failed again, and her only out was escape. She had run away from Alan to Golden, but in reality, all she'd done was run away from herself.

Kay pushed herself out of the rocker and looked around the room once more. She felt sad, but relieved in a way, as if she had purged all the memories. She realized that before Sean's death her marriage had been too perfect, a lovely jewel without a flaw. Because she and Alan were such a terrific couple they'd never had to resolve the darker sides of their natures.

But there was nothing wrong with her, she thought as she left the room and closed the door. There was nothing so terrible that love couldn't fix it. She and Alan had the kind of bond that was going to overcome the past and make their future something to rejoice in.

She walked out of their house, blinking in the bright afternoon sun. She had come out of a dark tunnel into sudden blinding light, and it was a shock, of course, but not a bad one. She could take it.

She smiled as she sat down on the porch, looking out toward the docks. Finally she wasn't afraid anymore. And if she had faced the truth alone, now she could face it with Alan.

Chapter Ten

She waited for him until nine-thirty, enjoying the quiet and relaxing back into the feeling of being in their house again. She flipped through a novel without absorbing any of it, went to the window every time a car passed and finally decided to go back to Erica's and pack her things.

Since she was moving back in with her husband, she didn't want to do it haphazardly. She didn't want him to just find her there, and she didn't want to sneak in like a thief in the night. No, she was going to return proudly, happily. She'd go over the next morning when she knew he'd be in and tell him, bags in hand, that she was home for good.

She woke up on Saturday feeling jubilant and quickly got her things together. But when she walked out into the living room to start the coffee, she found her sister mooning around, very restless and blue. She didn't have the heart to spring the news on Erica when she saw how lonely she looked. It was clear that she missed Mark. Also, Kay felt that her decision to go home again was between her and her husband. She wanted to get back to Sausalito that morning without Erica's encouragement, pressuring or cajoling. And she wanted to go as soon as possible.

When Erica pleaded with her to come shopping she nearly said no, but she couldn't bear seeing the downcast expression on her sister's face.

"Please," Erica repeated. "I feel like a stuffed pepper—I'm busting out of all my clothes. Anyway, there's something I have to discuss with you."

"We've got to be back by lunchtime," Kay said quickly, remembering that Alan occasionally played racketball on Saturday afternoons. If he had a game planned for that day, she was definitely going to see to it that he had something better to do—spend the day with her. Besides, she hated shopping on Saturday because the stores were always mobbed.

They wandered up Union Street, window-shopping and chatting casually, just two sisters out together. Yet there was an undercurrent of tension and anxiety between them.

"I talked to Mark last night," Erica said as they walked into a fashionable maternity store. "You'll never believe this, but he's enrolled in a child-birthing class in Minnesota. They didn't want to take him because he didn't have a partner, but he yelled and screamed and finally the instructor said *she'd* be his partner." Erica giggled and pulled a pair of baggy corduroys with a front stretch panel from the rack. "He's clearly the first man anywhere to do this."

"I don't get it," Kay said, her mind elsewhere. "Is this a sympathetic gesture? So he can feel he's doing something at the same time you're doing it?"

"Maybe." Erica pursed her lips as if deciding whether or not to tell her sister. "But he just may get back sooner than September as originally scheduled. He might be here for the birth, maybe even to help me through the last stages of my pregnancy. Kay, I love him. Please try to understand and be happy for me."

Kay turned to her with an expression of surprise on her face. "Well, I . . . That's great."

Erica snatched a few more items and started for the dressing room, as if suddenly afraid to discuss the subject any further.

Kay stayed where she was, feeling odd and left out. At first she had been resistant to the very idea of Erica's being a mother. But then she had grown to look forward to sharing Erica's pregnancy with her. But now, with Mark coming back . . . She felt a pang of something like jealousy, vaguely akin to what she'd felt while looking at the lamp Alan had bought without her.

"How's this?" Erica came to the door of the dressing room wearing a voluminous batik caftan with a big matching scarf wrapped around her blond curls. "Very African princess, don't you think?" She whirled around and modeled the dress for Kay.

"Very. I like it."

"Come on in and look at the rest. I'm getting bleary from having to make choices," Erica insisted.

Kay walked back to the small room and sat on one of the two stools in front of the mirror. "I went to Sausalito," she murmured as her sister pulled the dress over her head. She hadn't planned to reveal this, but it slipped right out.

"You what? When?" Erica's head appeared from under the folds of fabric.

"Yesterday. I walked into Sean's room and sat in the rocker where I used to nurse him. Oh, Erica . . ." Kay's hazel eyes grew misty. "I miss him. And I miss Alan."

Erica sat on the other stool and took Kay's hand. "Of course you do. That's why you have to go back."

"It took me so long to figure out that Sean's death didn't mean the death of our marriage." Kay shook her head. "But I was so terrible to Alan the last time we were together that I don't know if I can ever make him understand."

"Try," Erica urged, starting to get dressed in her own clothes again. "Don't wait. Do it today. Before it's too late."

Kay nodded and handed Erica her blouse. "I was planning to go this morning. Then you insisted we go shopping, and you looked so . . . so ghastly I couldn't say no. How *are* you doing, anyhow? Are you really okay?"

"Sure I am, sis. That was just a little deception," Erica confessed guiltily. "I wanted to spend some time with you so I could tell you about Mark coming back. I know he's not exactly your favorite person and I thought you'd get upset about it."

"Well, you were wrong." Kay smiled. "I'm very happy for you." She kissed her sister lightly on the forehead. Are you buying any of these?"

"Nope. Can't afford them. I'm borrowing all of Lena's maternity clothes." She started out of the dressing room.

"You take the cake!" Kay shook her head, unable to be annoyed at her crazy sister.

"Sounds like a good idea." Erica grinned mischievously. "Except I shouldn't eat cake. How about lunch? After all, now that you're moving back in with Alan, I won't get to see much of you. Boo-hoo!" She gave Kay a playful poke and Kay had to laugh, throwing her arms around Erica and squeezing her tight.

At five o'clock, Kay's cab pulled up in front of their house in Sausalito. The clanging of the sailboat riggings wafted up the hills to her where she stood looking down over the bay and the San Francisco waterfront beyond. A gusty breeze whipped her hair back as she emerged from the cab. She walked bravely to the front porch and stopped, fingering the key in her pocket.

Glancing around the side to the carport, she noted that the maroon Subaru was sitting right where it should have been. He was home. Yes, a light was on in the kitchen at the back. Probably making dinner. Dinner for one? she wondered anxiously. The most awful and embarrassing thing she could imagine would be walking in on Alan entertaining someone—male or female, or worse, some old friends of theirs.

Well, there was no way of knowing anything if she just stood there on the porch. But should she let herself in or ring the bell? She felt a little funny about just barging in after all this time. She reached up to press the doorbell, then stopped again. If this really was her home, and if she'd come back to resolve things, it was time to stop acting like a stranger. Taking the key from her pocket, she took a deep breath, then slipped it into the lock, turning the bolt. It gave with a loud click. But before she could twist the knob it turned in her hand and the door opened wide.

Alan was standing there in the dark hallway, his blue oxford shirt open to the waist and his feet bare under his navy twill slacks. He gazed down at her in complete amazement.

"I heard the cab drive up, so I came and looked through the peephole. I'm glad you used the key, that you didn't ring the bell."

Kay nodded and licked her lips, wondering what was going on in his mind as he looked at her, his deep brown eyes taking her in like a painting he particularly admired.

Alan looked down at his bare feet. "I was about to take a shower," he said, "but it can wait. Will you come in?"

"That's why I came." She laughed, thinking that was a stupid thing to say. She felt awkward and rather foolish, but very determined as she followed him in. He picked up her suitcases and brought them into the hallway. He didn't comment on them, but just kept walking into the living room.

He turned on the lamps on either side of the couch and indicated that she should take a seat.

"Well . . ." they both said at once.

Kay sighed and looked at the coffee table, unable to meet his questioning gaze. "I came to talk about Sean," she said. "I'm ready." The words had come out all run together as one sound and she worried that he hadn't been able to understand them, but the look of relief and joy on his face told her differently.

She couldn't sit still, so she got up and paced the room. "Yesterday I came here alone to look around. I had to see if I still belonged here."

"And do you?" he asked solemnly, not wanting to make the decision for her.

"I think . . . All I know is that I have to put Sean's death behind me and forget about it. Except that seems impossible. Everything I see or hear or touch reminds me of him, of the plans we had for him. And our whole marriage was bound so tightly around him."

"But it wasn't based solely on him, for heaven's sake," Alan cut in. "We were together for almost eight years before he was born."

"That was different!" she exploded, turning to him.

"Yes, it was. You know, when you went to Golden, I had plenty of time to see what being alone meant, and what loneliness felt like. I began thinking what would have happened to us if we'd had a handicapped child. We would have loved him just as much as we did a healthy baby like Sean, but we would have known he would be with us for a short while, so we would have mourned a little every day. With Sean, we had to do it all at once."

"I see what you mean." Kay nodded. She'd never thought about that.

"Kay, you don't have to forget him—that's the point. Not a day goes by when I don't think about Sean, not a night when I don't sit out there counting stars and looking for him someplace above the moon. But thinking about him—and talking about him as we're doing now—that's what keeps him alive, so he can never die. *Not* to talk about him, to avoid his death, that'll bury him for certain."

Kay looked at this man standing across the room from her, and a new spark of love burst forth in her heart. How did he know all this, how could he be so wise?

"Did that time away from me help?" he asked, not moving from his place on the couch. "Was it the tonic you needed?"

"No," she admitted. "Not at all. I just kept blaming myself over and over, and somehow I figured you missed Sean more than you missed me, so it would hurt to have me back and not him. That's why I stayed out there so long."

"Oh." He ran his hands through his curly dark hair and clenched them behind his neck. "I have to tell you that I was furious with you then. I'd been abandoned by my son, in a way, and then, to top it off, I was abandoned by my wife. For a while I simply couldn't handle it. Losing both of you at once was too much. I kept imagining you starting over with someone else and I'd want to put my hand through a door. You seemed so above it all, so cold and clinical, as though you could pick up a new life and drop the old one like a hot potato."

"Is that how I seemed to you?" she cried. She was horrified by the picture, and his words brought home another problem she'd been unwilling to face. He'd mentioned "someone else." Should she tell him about Johnny? It seemed so insignificant in the context of their relationship, but after all, it had meant a lot to Johnny. He'd even threatened to come to California to get her.

Oh, no! Kay thought in the midst of her growing confusion. Well, naturally, he wouldn't come. And telling Alan would only upset him.

"I wasn't really like that, Alan. I just held all my feelings in. They were there, though." Neither of them had moved, and she realized that she would have to go to him. She went and sat beside him on the couch but didn't touch him, letting him get used to the idea of her proximity.

"That whole time," he said, looking at her with a troubled expression on his face, "it seemed like I was the only one feeling the pain—I was the only one really mourning. That was a terrible feeling, Kay."

She studied his face, the sharp eyes boring into her consciousness, telling her that he would never again allow himself to be denied or rejected. It was vividly clear to Kay how much was at stake, how much she'd abandoned and would now have to reclaim.

"It seems stupid to say this now," she murmured, "but I felt the same way, trapped and alone with my grief. I couldn't see you standing there with open arms." The hollowness that had gnawed at her for months seemed ready to evaporate, if only he would reach out for her. They sat together, taking in each other's pain and emptiness. Then, at last, he offered his hand, palm up. It was such a simple gesture, but endowed with so much meaning.

"They're still open for you, if you're willing." The touch of his hand burned through her like a raging fire. She was instantly aroused and yet she felt that this wasn't right. It wasn't like the night when they'd gone to the hotel, when the need for physical contact had been so strong that it had had to be acknowledged. This was something different, something deeper, and Kay didn't want sex to change that. She got up and walked across the room.

"I am willing," she said, turning back to him. There was only one doubt in her mind now, and that was due to the fact that Alan hadn't yet told her that he loved her. Of course, she'd made that nearly impossible for him, but it was something she had to hear.

"Then come to me." He stood up, his eyes yearning, hungry for her.

"Alan, I . . ."

He wouldn't let her hesitate. He stalked across the room toward her, and it seemed to her that he grew more powerful and determined with each step. She stood, mesmerized, unable to move, unable to resist when he grabbed her wrist and pulled her close, parting the lapels of her coat with his free hand. He bent his head to her throat and rained kisses on the soft white skin, making Kay's flesh tingle and glow with excitement. As she arched away a moan escaped her lips. There was no turning back from the pulse in her blood that urged her on, crying out for more.

Slowly he unbuttoned her sheer white blouse. When it lay open he quickly undid the clasps of her bra, freeing her full breasts to his touch. He didn't have time to undress her but, instead, dropped his mouth lower to caress first one, then the other nipple with his tongue. She shuddered wildly, wanting to be free of her clothing, but he wouldn't let her go, nor did he make a move to help her. He kept up the pressure of his hands, sliding them lower on her hips while his mouth moved to one breast and his agile tongue circled it languorously.

Her weight sagged against him, pulling them both to the floor. Only then, as he laid her back gently on the thick white shag rug, did he ease the coat and blouse together off her body. Her hands were free to explore and they fumbled for a moment with his belt buckle before succeeding. He pressed down on her and she could feel the strength of him against her thigh. He rolled away for a brief instant so that she could unzip his pants, and then he stood up, naked before her.

She had never seen anything so magnificent, he was both the man she had known and loved before, and the deeper, wiser person he had become. His lower legs were golden tan and corded with muscles, leading up to powerful thighs and a narrow waist. The curly hair was matted to his chest with perspiration, and the silver strands glinted in the lamplight at her. His angular, bearded face was filled with a passion so urgent that she couldn't look into his eyes long for fear of being totally engulfed by it.

"Let me," he whispered, kneeling beside her. He slid her tapered black slacks off and thrust them aside, letting his hands roam over her breasts and stomach, moving lower, to her tender inner thighs. She reached for him, gasping for air, and he closed the distance between them, joining with her so effortlessly that she was astonished to realize that they were together.

He moved in her slowly, altering the rhythm whenever he wished to see her lovely face charged with a new emotion. He rose up from her once and tears filled her eyes because she couldn't stand to have him that far away. They rolled over, not even feeling it when they collided with an end table. But then, when the lamp fell over and broke, they both burst out laughing. It was Alan's new lamp. The mood shifted abruptly, and for a brief instant they were back to reality.

"Hey, you, watch the furniture," Alan growled.

"Your fault—you're bigger than me," Kay protested.

They kissed, their lips first brushing and then clinging, like their entwined bodies. Kay felt herself lifted somewhere above the floor. She was floating with him, racing through space, ducking around corners of the universe and playing hide-and-seek with the moon. The tide of desire rose in her and carried her further, so that she heard only his voice urging her on, taking her to new heights. She sobbed out her joy and he held her tightly, joining with her and lifting them both even higher. They passed over the edge of time and let gravity take over. Finally they were still.

Kay must have slept, because when she opened her eyes he was leaning on one elbow, gazing down at her with great tenderness. She blinked and smiled, then lifted her arms to bring his head down for a kiss. He ran his hands through her ash-blond mane and hugged her, rubbing his body against hers.

"I'll never be cold again," she sighed happily.

"I'll see to that," he promised.

A breeze wafted through the open window and they let it caress their sweating bodies. Kay looked out into the maze of stars above them. Each one looked brighter, clearer than it had before. "Alan," Kay whispered, "can I sleep over?"

He threw back his head and laughed, a warm, delighted sound. "Urchin, I thought you'd never ask."

They spent Sunday together. They didn't talk about much, simply tried to enjoy each other. When Kay first woke in her own bed, sliding along the cool sheets to reach her husband's body, she thought she was dreaming. Maybe the whole thing had been a dream and when she woke it would be to the sound of Sean's cooing in the next room.

But when she reached full consciousness she remembered everything. It was all right to be there, she thought with wonder, looking over at the handsome man sleeping beside her, his long lashes fluttering on his cheeks. This was where she was meant to be. The Alan and Kay who had existed before were only for practice—this was the real thing.

They made French toast and ate on the back deck. They went for a long bicycle ride and skipped lunch to make love again in a quiet cove on a deserted road overlooking the bay. When they got home they played records and sat peacefully on the couch to read.

It was odd, not like being married again, although it was clear that they were both enjoying themselves. But something hadn't clicked yet between them, Kay thought. Alan was wary of her, and as much as he tried to woo her with words and caresses, now part of him held back from being hurt. In a way, things were too idyllic, almost too easy, and she was wary of the feelings that made her want to ignore the reality of the situation—they were still separated in some important way.

Perhaps it would just take some more time before things became like they were, she thought at first. But deep down she knew that it was more complex than that, and this time she wasn't going to stubbornly tough it out alone.

Kay called Dr. Teller's office Monday morning and wangled an appointment for that very afternoon. She simply had to take every step possible, understand every facet of what had changed both her and Alan irrevocably. For better or worse.

The waiting room was empty when she walked in at four-thirty. Kay pushed a painted go-cart out of the way and picked up a doll and a teddy bear from one of the chairs so that she could sit down. The room was painted off-white and decorated with cutouts of animals and flowers. Sean had never minded coming here, she recalled, because there was so much to play with and so many new friends to make. That included the pediatrician, Dr. Sanford Teller.

When the doctor came out personally to greet her, she stood up and took his hand. He certainly didn't look like someone a child would immediately take to—thin and ascetic-looking with shaggy straight reddish hair that was fast going gray and thick glasses that obscured the warmth in his gray-green eyes. But his decidedly no-nonsense manner could vanish when he had a little boy or girl on his knee telling him where it hurt. In Sean's case, of course, there had been nothing he or anyone could have done.

"Come in, Dr. Devore," he said briskly. "I'm happy you wanted to see me. How's your husband?"

"He's . . ." She couldn't equivocate in front of this man. "We've been separated. We're trying getting together again, but . . . well, we keep holding back. I think I've pushed him into a corner."

"Do you think it's entirely your fault?" He led her into his consultation room and offered her the "grown-up" chair beside the tiny rocker reserved for whatever child had come in for an examination. The room was very quiet, with only the sound of burbling bubbles emanating from the aquarium on the far wall. Dr. Teller, Kay had been surprised to learn, was a collector of exotic fish.

"Women who've been through your experience always say it's their fault, did you know that?" He sighed, sitting behind his big desk. "There's this ingrown maternal guilt that overrides everything. The man never feels that way."

Kay settled herself back farther in her chair. "No, Alan didn't. With him it was more disbelief—like, how could this have happened to us?"

"Does he still feel that way? It's been . . . let's see, about six months since Sean died." The doctor peered at her anxiously.

"I guess not. I know he believes it, but he's better about realizing that Sean's life . . . How can I put this?" She stopped for a moment. "He says it's like a shooting star, you know? Its presence is still with you, even after it falls to earth."

The doctor leaned back in his chair. "Well, that's very poetic, and if it helps him that's fine, but I take it that you wouldn't be here if it helped you. Look, to be perfectly blunt about it, death is a fact. We all know we're going to die."

"But a healthy child—" Kay protested.

"Or a healthy parent," the doctor pointed out. "Have you ever known someone, strong as a horse, in the prime of life, who keels over the next day of a heart attack?"

Kay looked shocked. She got up and turned her back to the doctor as her eyes filled with tears. "My father," she murmured. "Two years ago."

"There you are. Now you'll tell me it's different with an infant. As much as you dreaded the idea, you expected your father to die before you. We expect to mourn our parents, because when they leave us, they've usually completed their cycle of living. It's as if they're passing on the mantle to us and saying, 'Now it's your turn to be the parent.' That's totally different from when your healthy baby dies unexpectedly. But crib death is no respecter of life. It's a horror, and it kills. What you have to do is realize that it hasn't killed you or your husband. Or, most likely, any other child the two of you might have at some point in the future."

Kay turned back to him, a fierce look in her green eyes. "But you can't promise that. And you can't promise that Alan or I might not be so scared that it's a gene or something the other one is carrying that we wouldn't be good parents to our next child. That it might be easier not to have children. You can't give me any guarantees."

"I'm not God." He shrugged. "Naturally, I can't. I can tell you it isn't genetic, and I can make available to you the best equipment we've got to ensure against its happening again. Do you want to hear about that?"

Kay paused, then nodded in the affirmative. Going back to Alan meant many different things, and one thing they would have to face was the idea of having another child. Their marriage was a partnership with dozens of interlocking facets. They helped each other with their careers, with housework, with their own parents and siblings, and together they carved out new areas to explore when they were ready. They both felt strongly about children—they'd wanted more than one. "Tell me," she said.

"We have an impedance monitor that we rent to parents who have lost one baby to SIDS. The next child is kept on the machine for a year whenever he's asleep or lying in his crib, with leads from the chest and mouth to check on heart rate and respiration. Someone has to be within earshot of the monitor at all times, because if it goes off, indicating that there has been some change—any change—in regularity, you have to jump in and give mouth-to-mouth resuscitation quickly. You have to shake the baby hard, get him not to succumb, start the systems working again. Now, I have to warn you, Dr. Devore, machines are machines and they're faulty, or they record things we don't intend them to measure. Many times they go off because the child has rolled over and disconnected a lead. It's the most harrowing and terrifying thing in the world to have that monitor go off for any reason, but a false alarm makes it worse."

Kay shook her head. "But we'd have to have one?"

"There's nothing else right now." The doctor shrugged. "And something is better than nothing. It could save a life. Your next child's life."

Kay rubbed her eyes, shaking off the doctor's tough, undaunted words. It was all so complicated. All she wanted to do was live a normal existence with a wonderful man and a terrific kid. Why was that so difficult? Dr. Teller didn't give her concern *or* sympathy—he just doled out the facts like bitter pills.

"I can see what's on the tip of your tongue. You're going to say that I don't really understand what you've gone through, are still going through. You're right, I'm not a woman and I've never known the pain and joy of childbirth. Nor, I might add, has your husband. But I have known other couples who have come out on the other side of crib death. Give me a little credit for my experience, will you?"

"What happened to them? The others?" Kay asked anxiously.

"Some snapped right back. In other cases the husband couldn't take it and ran off because he couldn't be supportive of his wife. In one instance, I remember, the couple wanted to burn all the baby's clothes and toys and furniture—thought they had to be contaminated. I told them they were out of their minds!" He gave a short laugh. "I've known couples who vowed never to have another child and, I might add, their sexual relationship went down the drain. But," he concluded, "in many cases the couple will cry it out, talk it out and, after a couple of years or so, they'll conceive again. And generally, I'd say, if they can get over their protectiveness, they're better parents because they've known the real meaning of loving and letting go."

Slowly Kay nodded. Her palms were damp with perspiration. "I think I'm beginning to understand now, doctor," she said.

"If we knew all the answers, Kay, and we knew the limits of our own lives and those of the people we love best, what would be the point? There has to be some mystery. That's what it's all about. Now, get out of here before I start preaching."

He walked her to the door and let her out, leaving her with a new sense of possibility. All her worrying and hiding and running away hadn't accomplished anything except to lead her further from the one person she desperately needed.

"There has to be some mystery," she repeated to herself over and over as she left Dr. Teller's office. Yes, that was probably true, although her scientific mind rebelled against the very notion. But if she were too good a detective, if she cleared up the mystery, she might lose what was most precious to her. Somehow she would have to let things happen to her, instead of controlling them. Somehow she would have to find her way back into Alan's heart for good.

Chapter Eleven

"I think this stuff is wonderful, Kay." Her supervisor, Dr. Kalens, looked at the rough draft of her presentation with unsuppressed glee in his eyes.

Kay laughed modestly. "I'm glad you're pleased with the results."

"Who would have thought that sea urchins could have provided all this? I'd like to see you start on a big project next year with some of the people at Berkeley. No reason why we can't work something out—it's done all the time at Harvard. Think about what you'd like to do and let me know. Anytime, Kay." He fairly bounced to the door of her lab, then turned and winked at her. "Whatever did it, and I'm not going to ask, I thank my lucky stars that you've come back to us for real. These past few weeks you've seemed very focused, Kay. I'm delighted."

Kay shook her head in amusement as she watched David walk out of the lab. He treated her as if she were a successful experiment that had netted the proper data. Actually, she marveled, sticking her notes in a manila folder and marking it for the typist, she was astounded that she'd had the concentration lately to complete anything.

"Kay?" Ada came through the swinging door looking very preoccupied. "Someone here to see you. I told him to wait in the corridor."

"Okay." She put down her pen and went out into the hallway, where she spotted a wiry young man wearing a baseball cap peering through the glass window of the next lab. "Yes, may I help you?"

The man turned around with a smile and came toward her with his hands outstretched.

"Mark!" she exclaimed. "Mark Sabia. But I thought Erica said you'd be in Minneapolis till—"

"It's a surprise. She doesn't know I'm back yet."

Kay gave him a quizzical look. What was her sister's boyfriend doing here? Why had he come to see her before Erica? She couldn't help but be a little suspicious. "Want to come into my office for a cup of coffee? I was just about to have some," she offered.

"That'd be great." He pulled off his cap and rumpled his hair, looking for all the world like a little boy desperate for approval. They walked down the hall to her small cubicle and she led him inside.

"Well, how've you been?" she asked awkwardly, pouring two cups from the small electric pot she kept by her window.

"Great. Really." His tentative manner clearly indicated that he was unsure of what kind of reception Kay would give him. After all, the last time they'd been together she'd nearly bitten his head off. She thought about her whole lecture on commitment and love and she winced inside. Who was she to tell anyone about love?

"I . . . uh, I guess you're wondering what I'm doing here," he began.

"Yes, actually, I am." She leaned back in the seat behind her cluttered desk and put her feet up in the open bottom drawer.

"I couldn't stay away from Erica." Mark shrugged, his earnest face alive with intense emotion. "See, I missed her terribly and even though we'd talked the whole thing out like sensible people, going on about where I was in my career and how good the thing in Minneapolis was for me, well, I just couldn't stop my feelings. I had to be with her now, while she's . . . at this particular time." Mark faltered, afraid to say "pregnant" in front of Kay. She picked up on it at once.

"Hey," she said softly, wondering how crazy she'd seemed to him that night that he wouldn't even mention the word. "It's all right. I'm coping a lot better now. You can say it."

"Oh." He smiled with relief. "That's great, Kay. Yeah, so, I really felt strongly about going through the pregnancy with her. It's not something someone should do alone."

Kay's heart went out to him. "I can't tell you how happy it makes me to hear you say that. And the only thing I can't figure out is why you're sitting here in my office when you should be rushing to her side."

Mark laughed appreciatively. "I wanted your approval first."

"Mine?" Kay asked in surprise. "Well, you've got it—wholeheartedly. I think what you two are doing is wonderful. And I think it's more wonderful that you came back early."

"Boy, have *you* changed your tune! Last time I saw you it looked like you thought Erica and I were plain cuckoo."

Kay licked her lips, turning to stare out the window at the planetarium across the way. "We're all cuckoo. But that's part of the deal, isn't it? What works for one couple would never work for another—that's the big mystery of love." She smiled when she said the word, thinking of herself and Alan. "Your love works for you. Despite the fact that neither of you has a steady job and you're separated a lot of the time, you still love each other enough to get through all that. There aren't many people who have what you have," she added softly.

Mark got up and came over to take her hand. He pressed it warmly between his. "Thank you, Kay. That means a lot to me."

"Really?" Kay was slightly surprised to hear that a free spirit like Mark needed her approval so badly.

"Sure. After all, you are my future sister-in-law."

It took a moment for this announcement to register. Then she leaped from her seat, laughing, to embrace him. "That's fantastic! Congratulations! When did you pop the question?"

"Hey, I couldn't do something as important as that on the phone, Kay," he objected.

"You mean . . . she doesn't know?" Kay was incredulous.

"No. Although she's a pretty smart girl—she might suspect. I can't tell you what devious tricks I've had to use to creep around San Francisco without her sniffing me out. I've been in town now for two days making arrangements," he confessed.

"Sounds like you're planning to get down on one knee and make an old-fashioned proposal," Kay teased.

"Well, why not? But see, before I did that I had to straighten out my work situation. I mean, if I'm going to turn into a husband and father in the flick of an eye I've got to make sure I can handle it financially. What I did was send out a barrage of résumés from Minneapolis. The employment picture around here is lousy for anybody, let alone an actor, but I did get a couple of bites before I flew back here. As luck would have it, I landed a half-time job yesterday."

"That's incredible," Kay marveled, greatly impressed with his determination. In a way he reminded her of Alan when he was just out of school and looking for work.

"It is, kind of. But I figured the fates were with me. Since I fell in love with Erica, all sorts of good things have happened to me."

"Well, don't keep me in suspense—what's the job?" Kay demanded.

"Lady, you are looking at the Mission Street Circus School's new juggling coach. And with the half-time hours I'll be able to pay the rent and pursue my acting career at the same time." He looked pretty pleased with himself, and Kay couldn't blame him.

"That's terrific." She smiled.

"Now, wait, I'm not finished. I told you I was on a roll. I also got a callback for a super part in a new play—all in the same day. Is the kid lucky or what?" He stuck out his hand and she shook it vehemently.

"I have just one question. When in the name of heaven are you going to tell Erica all this good news?"

He grinned and shrugged, then sat back down in the chair facing her. "That's why I'm here, Kay. See, I've given this a lot of thought, and even though Erica and I sometimes pride ourselves on being unconventional, well, I think marriage is enormously important, a sacred tradition, even. I want to do it right."

She peered into his shining eyes and a warm affection for Mark gripped her. She was proud of him and proud of her sister. It was a very good feeling. "Yes, and what can I do for you?"

He reached into his pocket and pulled out a small box. "I want your honest opinion. Don't try to spare my feelings, okay? I want the truth." He snapped open the cover to reveal a diamond engagement ring. "Is this good enough for Erica? It's such a tiny chip of a stone that I'm almost embarrassed to give it to her, but I just couldn't swing anything bigger right now. I even had to throw in my old silver-and-turquoise bracelet to make the deal." He laughed nervously. "I mean, do you think it might be better to give her nothing now and tell her she's got my love and that when I have some money I'll buy the ring? What do you think?"

Kay just rolled her eyes to the ceiling. Men could be such idiots sometimes. "It's a gorgeous ring, Mark," she told him. "The size of the stone is completely insignificant—don't you know that? To Erica it'll look as big as the moon. It's what it means that counts, and the fact that it's from your heart."

"Really?"

"Really," she affirmed.

He jumped out of his seat and reached the door in a second. "Then I'm on my way." He was halfway into the corridor when he stopped himself with a laugh. "Terrific. I forgot to ask where she is today."

"Home." Kay grinned. "She had a doctor's appointment this morning, so she couldn't take any temp work today. If you hurry you can catch her before she leaves for rehearsal."

"Fantastic!" Mark beamed, lunging at Kay to give her a hug. "Hey, have a spectacular day, will you?" he yelled. Then he was out the door, looking about as gleeful and excited as a kid on Christmas morning. His enthusiasm was infectious, Kay realized as she closed the door and walked to the window. She felt better about herself, about everything. Certainly about having Mark Sabia in the family.

She glanced at her own engagement ring, nicely couched above her wedding band on her finger. It was, as Mark had said, a sacred tradition. These rings were the symbols of something so precious and important that it was difficult to think that there were people out there who believed in divorce.

The view from Kay's window was a busy one, with dozens of people leaving the Academy buildings for a walk on the plaza or a quick lunch on the steps. Tourists were enjoying the beautiful spring weather, letting their kids climb on the animal sculptures or sitting comfortably in groups to talk. Somehow the sight brought Kay up short. This was real life—people going about their business, working, eating, loving, considering marriage, even.

She could scarcely wait for the day to be over so that she could climb into the car beside her husband and speed toward home. When five-thirty came Kay was already on the plaza steps, waiting for him.

"Hi, early bird," he said lightly as he kissed her and took her arm. "Wait till I tell you about the mammoth formations on the asteroid we're looking at. Perhaps over a wonderful fish dinner, overlooking the bay, with an attentive maître d', what do you say?"

"Let's just get a pizza and then go home and have a quiet evening, Alan. If you don't mind," she added quickly.

"Mind? How could you ask if I'd mind?" Suddenly he looked upset, and she could tell that they had a way to go before their ideas and feelings were completely in sync again.

"You know what I meant," she said lamely. "Oh, stop at Martin's, would you? I dropped off some of your shirts the other day."

"That was sweet of you," he said quickly.

She turned to him, a frustrated smile on her face.

"Alan, quit it, all right? I always took your shirts. This is not an act worthy of the Nobel Prize."

"I only meant . . ." Then he laughed, realizing that now he was explaining. He reached across the seat and took her hand. "Why are we doing this?"

"Because." She smiled.

It happened again with the pizza. He asked her what she wanted on it, and he knew—or should have known—that she only liked mushrooms and sausage. That was the way they'd ordered pizza for years, and she looked hurt that he felt he had to ask.

"It doesn't matter, Alan," she assured him later when they lay on the rug in front of the bay windows, looking out at the night sky. "That sort of thing is kid stuff, not what counts."

"It all counts," he told her quietly. Then he sighed and moved away. "I never thought this would take any effort at all. There we'd be, as much in love as ever."

She was silent then, wondering if he meant that he didn't love her the way he used to. It was stupid, and she was aware that she was creating problems, but the thought remained with her all night and all the next morning. He hadn't told her that he loved her since she had come back from Golden. That knowledge stuck in her throat like a pill that wouldn't go down.

By lunchtime the next day, though, she felt better. She kept reminding herself that they were working their way back together again and that these things took time. The important thing was that they were learning what their marriage was really made of. They were spending every waking minute exploring what they liked and disliked, hoped for and were afraid of. That was what made them a couple.

Finally it was twelve-thirty and Kay knew exactly what she was going to do. There was a smile on her face as she got out of the elevator on the first floor of Steinhardt and started for the door. Wouldn't Alan be surprised when she barged into his office and said, "I love you. How about lunch?" It didn't matter that he hadn't said it. She would say it first. They'd talk and gaze into each other's eyes. It wouldn't be like old times between them—it would be the start of a new understanding.

She crossed the plaza, starting for the planetarium on the other side. But as she passed the front door of the administration building a tall figure coming out caught her eye. She drew in her breath sharply as she recognized the floppy hair tucked behind his ears and the long, loping stride of Johnny Pallas.

"Oh, no," she murmured, frozen to the spot. She hadn't taken his ultimatum seriously, of course, but now she remembered all too well what he'd told her on the phone. "If I don't hear from you soon," he'd said, "I'm coming out to California to get you." And that was exactly what he'd done.

Johnny saw her at that instant and started running toward her, his arms outstretched. "Kay!" He folded her in a big bear hug and she submitted anxiously, quickly moving away as soon as he loosened his grip. They were both very much aware that this was the first time they had ever embraced. Johnny had a broad, childlike grin on his face as he stood back and held her at arm's length.

"I found you! I was just on my way to your lab."

"Johnny, I can't believe you did this," Kay sputtered. "You should have called before showing up." She felt cranky and annoyed with him for disrupting her day, for messing up her life, but she couldn't really show her anger in the face of his boyish delight.

"Hey, I waited long enough. I wasn't about to stop for a phone call. I thought long and hard about coming out here. Your mom kept telling me to forget it, but I had to see you and thrash this thing out in person. Phones are so lousy, you know? You look great!"

She sighed and glanced around, suddenly self-conscious about standing with him in the plaza. She wanted to get away before anyone saw them together. Clearly her plan for lunch was no longer a possibility.

"Why don't we take a walk?" Kay suggested, already walking away from the planetarium. "The Zoological Gardens aren't far—we can get a hot dog and talk." She kept trying to think of a nice way to let him down easy, but none of the pat phrases that came to mind seemed adequate. Johnny had helped her through the worst time of her life and it was her fault that she'd been too self-absorbed to see that he was falling in love with her. Now it was her job to make him understand.

As they started to walk Johnny looped an arm around her shoulder and she quickly drew away, steering them through a group of dawdling tourists.

He looked surprised, but kept his distance after that, biding his time. They strolled into the zoo and Kay found that her mind was a blank. She had no idea what to say to him.

"I'm crazy about zoos." Johnny walked ahead of her, over to the railing beyond which an enclosed series of rock formations formed a pen for the bears. Three large grizzlies were sunning themselves on the grass. "Isn't this place modeled on that zoo in Germany where the animals roam free?" he asked.

"That's it," Kay agreed, wondering why they were talking about zoos. "These moats protect them from the public."

"Too much!" Johnny laughed happily, leaning over the railing.

Kay couldn't help but see him for what he was at that moment: wide-eyed, overly enthusiastic, naive—more a boy than a man. There was no denying that he was very attractive—tall and muscular with a lean, unlined face like a movie cowboy's. But there was something missing from those blue eyes, the kind of depth of experience that Alan's possessed. Not that many women wouldn't find Johnny appealing. And for good reason—he was kind, good-natured, sympathetic and certainly persistent.

"So." He smiled, turning away from the bears and leaning back on his elbows to gaze at her. "Are you surprised?"

"You could have knocked me over with a feather. I never dreamed you'd really come all the way out here for—"

"For you?" Johnny interrupted. "Sweetheart,

you've got a lot to learn about Johnny Pallas. When he wants something he'll go to the ends of the earth to get it."

Kay turned and started to walk away, but he grabbed her arm. "Hey, don't do that," he said softly. "I know you feel something for me too, Kay."

She sighed and nodded. "I'm very fond of you. I'm grateful to you. You stood by me when I was a real basket case, Johnny. And you were a good friend. But that's all I feel. Really." She looked up into his eager face and was saddened to see that he didn't believe her.

"I'm going to stick around, Kay. I'm going to convince you of what you want, because I can see that you're still too confused to make decisions for yourself."

Her eyes flashed, warning him, but he didn't notice. "Come on," he said. "I see a hot-dog cart right over there, next to Monkey Jungle."

She went with him quietly, her mind a maze of imperatives. She had to be nice to Johnny; she had to get rid of Johnny; she had to see Alan.

"You grab that bench over there," Johnny instructed her. I'll get the hot dogs—mustard and relish on yours. And a ginger ale. See? I remember." He smiled confidently, pleased with himself.

Kay watched him walk over to get their lunches. It pained her to see him like that, all fired up to win her and woo her. The sad thing was that Johnny thought that true love was only remembering what Kay liked on her hot dog. The superficial knowledge he had of her likes and dislikes seemed like ignorance compared to the deep intimacy she shared with Alan. Naturally it was stupid to compare them, and yet she found herself doing it—their looks, their voices, the way they gazed appreciatively at her. In every category Alan was the winner, hands down.

"Here you are." Johnny handed her the hot dog, taking a seat beside her. "Eat up and I'll get you another. Or maybe you should take the afternoon off and show me the town. It's my first time in San Francisco—did I tell you? But I've been reading up, so I know everything I want to see. Fisherman's Wharf, the Presidio, Chinatown, the Coit Tower—all of it. All with you by my side, as my guide." He pressed closer and for a moment she was afraid that he was going to kiss her. But, sensing her mood, he just smiled and took a big bite of his frankfurter.

"Listen, Johnny," Kay began with a pang of anguish in her heart, "I know it must have looked like I ran out on you when I left Golden, and maybe you read more into that than you should have. How do I say this without sounding horribly selfish?" She crossed her legs, then uncrossed them. "Leaving had nothing to do with you. Nothing at all."

He was silent for a minute, taking this in. Then he went on eating thoughtfully. "I'm listening," he murmured.

"I was mixed up about me, about my marriage. But not because I'd ever remotely considered it a failing marriage. It was the best. And it can be again. You met me right after the most terrible thing that could ever have happened to a couple. Alan and I went through something I never told you about. You should know, though."

"I do, Kay. I know your son died," Johnny said quietly, taking her hand. "Your mom told me right before I called you. I wish I'd known before. It's not like I can make it up to you, of course, but I can make you forget."

"Johnny—" she began to protest, but he cut her off.

"It's like falling off that horse, Kay. You have to get back on, otherwise you'll live in fear all your life. I want to give you another baby, more than anything. And you aren't getting any younger, which makes it even more urgent that you come home with me now. I need you, sweetheart, and I can make you need me." His fierce gaze raked her face and she stood up, knocking her lunch aside in her haste to get away. How could he even have suggested such a thing? Clearly this man could never understand what made her tick.

"It's not like replacing a pet, Johnny. You're not dumb—you must know that," she said sharply. But as she spoke she saw that he didn't understand. No one—not him or Lena or Beatrice or even Erica—no one who hadn't gone through the horror of losing a child could ever comprehend. That was why Alan was the only person on earth who could really know her, could love the unfathomable, most mysterious and best-hidden parts of her character.

Johnny got up and steered her toward the next animal pen. "Look at that." He pointed to a high limb of the tree above them, where a chimp was meticulously grooming her little one. "I mean, isn't that what it's all about?" he asked earnestly. "There's nothing more important than two people who care for each other bringing a new life into the world. That can blot out all the pain and despair you've known."

Kay tried not to laugh at his feeble attempt to move her with his profound-sounding statement about monkeys and people and the Great Scheme of Things. She didn't want to seem condescending or critical, but there was an awful lot Johnny Pallas had to learn. "Come off it, Johnny," she said. "This is real life I'm talking about."

He looked stunned, as though the woman he was involved with had suddenly vanished, leaving Kay in her place. "How could you even suggest that I don't hurt for you? That I don't know exactly how you feel?"

"Because you don't," Kay said simply. "Look, I have to get back to work, Johnny. I'm not trying to be cruel, don't you see? It's just that my life is taking another turn now."

Without looking back she walked briskly away from him, surer than ever of the path she had chosen for herself. She was thinking so hard about her new course of action and how to approach Alan that she didn't even feel Johnny's hand on her elbow at first. She just kept walking.

"I'll sit in your office till you're finished this afternoon. I don't give up easily, Kay," he warned her.

She didn't respond but kept going. Was there no way to convince him? By the time they got back to her lab, Johnny had repeated his pleas at least five more times, and Kay was getting exasperated. She practically ran into her office for her lab coat, ignoring the strange look Ada gave her as Johnny followed her through the open door.

"All right, you listen to me." Kay turned on him. "You can't bully someone into doing whatever you want, Johnny, particularly when it comes to an emotional relationship. I don't like doing this—I feel lousy telling you to go take a hike, but you won't listen to reason. You put all the burden on me—coming out here after me, demanding that I change my life for you! It doesn't work that way, don't you see? Now, leave me alone!" She was close to tears when she finished, completely oblivious of Ada and Tommy, who were standing in the hall trying not to eavesdrop. But Kay felt miserable about rejecting another human being. She, who had known the deepest loss of love, was acutely sensitive to others going through the same thing.

Johnny grabbed her, and she pulled away and shook her head violently from side to side, which only made him press closer. "Dammit, Kay," he proclaimed, "I love you. I promise you this—I'm not going back to Golden without you."

If only he hadn't said the words she'd been longing to hear, though not from him. Johnny had told her that he loved her, and that had cut her to the very quick. From him it didn't mean anything; Alan was the person she had to hear it from.

Kay only knew that she had to get as far from him as she could. Wrenching herself out of his grasp, she staggered out the door, colliding with a hard thud against the shoulder of the person who had been waiting patiently to one side of the door.

She looked up and turned a sickly shade of gray as she realized that it was Alan. He had heard and seen everything.

His face was a mask of fury as he pushed her roughly aside. His mouth tightened as his deep brown eyes, now cold as ice, accused her.

"Alan—" she began.

"Never mind," he spat at her. "Just never mind!" He turned on his heel and stalked down the hall toward the stairs, his powerful back a massive angry emblem that told her exactly what he thought of her. He'd seen her in another man's arms, heard that the man was from Golden, where she'd spent three months. Time without him, time on her own, when she might have said and done things he could never know about. But up until now he had trusted her, had never even thought to question what experiences she might have had without him. In one brief instant she had obliterated his trust. In his mind she had betrayed him, and worse, she had lied.

Johnny saw the look on her face and knew better than to try to touch her. "Say you'll have dinner with me tonight, at least," he pleaded.

She didn't even have the strength to say no. "I'm married to that man," she whispered, looking down the corridor in the direction Alan had gone. "I love him, and I'll never let him go." She turned to Johnny, her green eyes bright with tears. "Do you read me?"

The hurt little boy before her shook his head sadly, proving to Kay once again that there was no contest. Johnny was a boy. Alan was a man.

"Go home." She sighed. "Go home and forget

about me." Her pained smile turned tender as she reached up to kiss him on the cheek.

He bit his lip and nodded solemnly. "You never looked at me the way you looked at him just now. I guess that look said it all."

He walked away quickly, giving her no opportunity to pity him. He'd get by.

But would she? She'd been so close to straightening things out with Alan, and now this had happened. In all their married life together neither of them had so much as glanced at another person. They didn't have to, because they fulfilled every one of each other's needs. Suddenly, in the brief space of a moment, Alan's trust and belief had been wiped away, to be replaced by that deadly green-eyed monster, jealousy.

Kay walked slowly back into her office. There had been a time, only weeks earlier, when she would have taken this as her ultimate defeat. She had given up trying to start over after Sean, had given up hope in her own ability to rebuild her marriage. But that was before. Now her future was spread out before her like a banquet, a huge feast that would feed and nurture her through the years. As long as she refused to give up—and as long as her love sustained her.

How would she convince Alan of that love? There was no way to know until she tried, and try she would—until she succeeded.

Chapter Twelve

Kay finished up in the lab at about six and changed into the fresh clothes she kept in her office closet. Not that she had any thought of appearing seductive that night; she just needed a change of attitude, and clothes never failed to do that for her. She felt exhausted and saw as she glanced at herself in her pocket mirror that there were shadows under her deep green eyes. Lack of sleep did nothing for her fair skin, just made her appear thinner and more drawn. Well, she hadn't had her eight hours for several nights running—she'd been thinking too hard to sleep much. But she had finally reached her decision: She had to confront Alan.

After she had slipped on the blue-and-white cotton blouse with big puffy sleeves and a pointed lace collar and a white skirt, then touched up her makeup and hair, she felt fresher, ready for anything. When she walked out the door at six-thirty she was a new woman.

There had never been such a lovely May evening, Kay mused as she strolled down the steps of the Steinhardt Aquarium. A perfect night for romance—or, she thought ruefully to herself, for a knock-down, drag-out battle for the man she loved. It wouldn't be easy; she didn't expect Alan to give an inch. She knew his rage—hadn't he almost destroyed her office once?—but it no longer terrified her. She knew how to deal with her own emotions more effectively, and that meant she could handle Alan's, too. It would be like that fairy tale in which the young hero was told by the princess's father that he could have her hand in marriage only if he could hold on to her through one entire night. Magically she changed into a fierce dragon, then a hissing snake, then a cruel vulture and, finally, a raging ball of fire. But the hero's love was pure and he knew that no matter what she looked like, she was the woman he loved. When the dawn broke, the creature in his arms changed back into the beautiful princess. He had conquered the impossible and won her forever.

As I'll win Alan, no matter how bad he gets, Kay vowed to herself.

She was on her way to the corner to catch the bus to Sausalito when she heard a car horn honk right behind her. She turned to see Mark waving her down from behind the steering wheel of Erica's dilapidated VW. Erica was languorously draped over the passenger seat.

"Hey, wait up!" Mark called, pulling to the curb and parking right in front of Kay.

Erica grinned at her sister as she opened the door and eased her way out, her left hand preceding her. "Say congratulations," she instructed, flashing her ring.

With a whoop of delight Kay embraced Erica and hugged her tightly. "Congratulations, for heaven's sake! Oh, sweetie, I'm really happy for both of you."

Erica glanced down at her protruding stomach. "The three of us, if you please. But listen, I'm not changing my name. Erica Rogers is becoming known in theatrical circles and I can't start all over again now."

"The baby," Mark explained, coming over to them, "will be known as Butch."

Kay laughed, but Erica rewarded him with a gentle bop on the head. "No, we're going to call her Amanda Rogers Sabia. Or perhaps Sabia-hyphen-Rogers, what do you say?"

"I like the Amanda part," Kay commented wryly. She was thrilled for them, but only half-concentrating. Her mind was really on Alan. "You two going out to celebrate?"

"Actually, we're going to the bookstore to stock up on childbirthing books. When classes start I want to be ready. Mark's already gone through the whole course in Minnesota, so he'll be terrific, but I don't know a thing."

Mark put his arm around his bride-to-be and gently kissed her forehead. "She'll be the rock of Gibraltar."

"I hope so," Kay muttered, still thinking of what she had to do that night. She glanced down the street and noticed the headlights of an approaching bus in the distance. "Look, you guys," she told them, "this is my bus; I've got to run. 'Bye."

Mark and Erica looked at each other, wondering what Kay's big hurry was and why she wasn't driving home with Alan. But there was no time for questions because Kay had already boarded the bus and paid her fare.

Things better work out the way I want them to, Kay thought to herself, *or I'll be sleeping in a hotel again tonight.* Then she took a seat in the back, where she could watch the lights of the Golden Gate twinkle like hundreds of little stars, almost close enough for her to reach out and touch them.

The house was dark when she got there; Alan wasn't home yet. A stray neighborhood cat meandered around the corner and came trotting over to her, meowing loudly. She was a pretty little thing, although very skinny, with sleek orange fur and bright topaz eyes. Kay patted her head and scratched between her ears, and the cat immediately lay down comfortably on the front steps.

Wouldn't it be nice if you could satisfy a person that easily? Kay mused, absently stroking the cat's fur. Just be nice to them, love them a little and they'd be yours. But with people there were hundreds of complications, and no sooner did you take care of one than another sprang up to replace it, rearing its ugly head to destroy the affection that had started to grow.

But that, of course, was what Dr. Teller had meant by the mystery of the whole thing. Why were people attracted to one another? Kay knew dozens of couples with problems, seemingly mismatched, fighting like cats and dogs—and yet they stayed together. Then there were others who looked on the surface like delighted, passionate lovers who would suddenly announce, out of the blue, that they were getting a divorce.

Kay leaned back and looked at the stars, their beauty shadowed by clouds. She wanted a little of that kind of beauty in her own life, and it seemed so difficult to get it. First her child had died, then she had nearly ruined her marriage, and, finally, another man had practically delivered the coup de grace. She thought fondly of Johnny, though. It really wasn't his fault that this had happened. And under other circumstances she would have dragged him over to the planetarium to introduce him to Alan as the good friend who'd been so helpful when she was in Golden.

Friends were important, dammit. It was odd, now that she thought about it, but since her marriage she'd cared a lot less about having friends she could rely on. Of course, as a couple she and Alan saw the Birches and the Villiers pretty regularly, but that was much more a social thing. Her friends, the people she could confide in and share things with, had sort of fallen by the wayside as she grew closer and closer to Alan. Erica was really the best woman friend she had now. But maybe being part of a couple did that to you—because people assumed they couldn't come between a husband and wife who had a "perfect" marriage. When she thought about it, Alan didn't really have anyone but her to call a best friend. Which was why he certainly should understand when she explained about Johnny.

Should. She laughed quietly to herself. Not *would.*

The sound of an approaching car made the cat jump up in fright and dart away. Kay steeled herself for what was to come. Somehow she knew that the car was the Subaru and that Alan was in it.

The headlights blinded her as he pulled into the driveway with an angry squeal of brakes. She sat still, waiting for him to walk up onto the porch. But for several agonizing minutes he just sat in the car, staring straight ahead through the windshield. Kay felt for him, for herself, for both of them. This was going to be very difficult.

At last, with a weary shake of his head, he got out, slamming the door behind him. The thick wooden columns of the porch kept him from seeing her immediately, but when he did, he stopped dead and glared at her, intense emotion seething in his sharp eyes.

"What are you doing here?" he growled, walking up onto the porch and towering over her.

"Well, I couldn't exactly leave things as they were," Kay said softly.

He looked her up and down, evaluating her. She had never been so exposed or vulnerable, and the terrible anger in his face frightened her, reminding her of the day when he had thrown the books to the floor in her office. But behind the anger she could see other emotions—hurt and pain. Kay knew that she would do everything in her power to assuage them, even if it cost her her own self-respect.

"I think there are a few misconceptions we have to clear up," she said when he didn't speak.

"No misconceptions. I got the picture. You picked up some lumberjack when you were staying in Golden and had a little fling. And from what I saw outside your office, that must have been *quite* a fling." He jerked his house key out of his pocket and rammed it into the lock. "You just had to lie to me, didn't you? Why didn't you simply come out and tell me you had an affair?"

"Because I didn't," she proclaimed hotly, following him into the front hall. "That man . . . that boy," she corrected herself, "was a good friend to me for three months. I was a puddle of self-concern and he just sat and listened. I never told him about Sean, mainly because I didn't feel it was anyone's business but ours. He simply knew something was terribly wrong with me and he tried to cheer me up."

"I'll bet he did." Alan stalked into the living room, shrugging off his jacket and throwing it over the nearest chair. He stood in the dark, staring out the window. "Now, why don't you get out of here and leave me alone?"

"I will not." She sat awkwardly on the hassock that went with the big chair, trying to think of a way to get it all straight. His anger seemed so impenetrable that she didn't know where to begin.

"Kay," Alan said with a sigh, running his fingers through his thick curls, "I've done a lot of thinking since I saw you in the corridor with that man. It's not only having an affair. God knows I would have been torn apart if you'd told me, but eventually I would have accepted it. It's the *not* telling, don't you see that? You've been doing this right along. You wouldn't talk about Sean's death. You wouldn't talk about our marriage. And now you hold back on telling me about another man. You're just a big bundle of secrecy—I feel like I've been married to a CIA agent! Everything gets covered up, tucked away in some nice little corner. Well, listen to me, lady!" He came around to her and yanked her upright, gripping her arms tightly. "I don't want a wife who keeps her life from me. That doesn't interest me in the slightest. Not anymore."

His voice rang with the fervor of his words and she looked at him in horror as she realized what he was saying. They had come so far together, and now he was chucking her out—maybe for good.

"Let me go," she said calmly. "You're hurting me."

He dropped her arms as though they had suddenly become too hot to touch, and the look on his face told her that he hadn't realized his own strength.

"You're all wrong about Johnny—that's his name, by the way. I didn't mention him because we had more important things to discuss. He simply wasn't relevant to us, Alan."

"Oh, I think he most certainly was!" he cut in with a scornful laugh.

"Will you shut up and hear me out!" She surprised herself as well as Alan by her tone of voice. She had never told him to shut up before, not in the nine years they had known each other so fully, so intimately. "Another reason I didn't tell you about him was that I thought you might jump to conclusions. And bingo, look at you—you don't bother to ask one question, you just assume that he and I were lovers. You have a horrible temper, Alan. How can I talk to you, tell you my 'secrets,' as you call them, when I think you may be about to fly off the handle? I'm not the only one to blame here."

He was taken aback by her accusation, and as he walked away his powerful shoulders slumped forward in self-defeat. She hated to see him that way.

"Am I making any sense?" she whispered.

"I simply don't know whether to believe you or not," he said hopelessly. He turned and stared into her face, willing an answer to appear there. "I thought a week ago that we had everything worked out. But I'd thought that before. I believe you're one thing, then I turn around and see that you're something entirely different. You never used to be a mystery. I knew everything about you, every move you'd make, every word you'd say. Now I find out I didn't know you at all."

She came to him, her hands outstretched. "That's the whole point, Alan. There has to be mystery. Don't accept me for what I was before Sean died, or even what I was yesterday. Oh, naturally I'm mostly the same old Kay, but I *have* changed, and so have you. That's what's been disturbing us, keeping us apart—the thought that it'll never be the way it was before. It can't be."

He seemed racked by torment, unable to decide whether he could live with what she was saying. But she knew that he wanted her, that he would never let her go. "Why did that guy follow you all the way from Golden?" he asked. "You must have given him some encouragement."

"He believed what he wanted to believe about me—just like you. He thought there was love between us when there was only friendship, and he was determined to come get me and make me see the light. Instead, I told him to go home. Alan," she nearly begged, "I never wanted another man. I only want you."

She reached for him, but he pulled away. "Do you? Do you really? I was ready to ask for a divorce."

She reeled away from him as though he'd hit her. "Oh, my God," she whispered. "Oh, no."

"You don't want one?"

"How can you ask me that?" She slumped down on the couch, hiding her face from him so he wouldn't see the bright tears about to spill over.

"I just don't know about us, Kay. Even if I believe you about that guy, how can I be sure we'll ever be happy again?" He sat on the opposite end of the couch, but he was miles away from her.

"There are no guarantees," she said. "Only good hard work. Only . . ." She was about to say "love," but caught herself in time.

"I don't want to live my life surrounded by ghosts, Kay. Not Sean's, certainly, and I'm afraid you'll never let him die."

She drew her breath in sharply. "You were the one who said that by keeping his memory alive, by not forgetting him, we could keep some part of him with us. That's all I want, Alan. Not to keep him enshrined like some kind of god. I've made my peace with his death, and all I want is to keep the good things he gave us."

"But do you want to go on?" Alan asked softly without looking at her. "Do you want to think about our future together?"

Before she could think of how to respond she heard the words coming from her own mouth. "I want to have another child. Your child."

Alan was silent, and she didn't dare to look at him. It was clear that he wanted to believe her, but he still couldn't be certain that someday, despite her trying, she wouldn't retreat into her own little world, shutting him out.

She eased herself off the sofa, bone-weary from emotional stress. It was the oddest feeling, as she stood up, as if the floor were rushing up to meet her. Suddenly she landed on it with a hard thump and opened her eyes to meet Alan's troubled gaze. He was bending over her, lifting her head.

"What happened?" she asked. She tried to raise herself up on one elbow, but he wouldn't let her move, pinning her in place with one hand across her chest.

"You stood up and passed out." He watched her closely.

"I haven't been sleeping awfully well," she admitted. "I've . . . uh, had a lot on my mind." She wanted to tell him that she had missed him, but she didn't dare.

He didn't say anything, just helped her slowly to her feet and steered her toward the bedroom. "I'll get you some warm milk while you undress. You always used to love that," he added.

"Alan, really, I'm fine. And I don't want to go to sleep right now. We were just in the middle of the most important discussion of our lives, for heaven's sake." She tried to push him away, but he already had her shoes off and was sitting her on the bed.

"It'll wait; it's waited this long, hasn't it? Go on, take your things off. Your nightgowns are . . . well, you know where they are." He laughed nervously, backing out of the room. "I'll get the milk."

She sat on the bed, debating with herself about whether she should stay now after what they'd just been through. It seemed so inappropriate after discussing infidelity and divorce and secrecy for her to be climbing into the bed they had shared for so many years. Naturally Alan would offer to sleep in the guest room and she would agree. Then, in the morning they'd meet over toast and coffee with tight little smiles. He'd ask her if she had slept well and she'd respond politely, and they'd be right back where they started, splitting up for good.

Or would she keep up the act? The old Kay would have clung to that kind of pretense. The new, more open Kay would undoubtedly say, "I didn't sleep a wink because I wasn't lying in your arms." But, once again, that kind of dumb comment put her in the driver's seat. Maybe he'd been serious about divorcing. Maybe the cold, hard truth was that he didn't want her anymore.

She sighed and unbuttoned her blouse, walking on shaky legs to the closet to hang it up. She unzipped her skirt and put that away, then tossed her beige silk half-slip over it on the hanger. It had been a joke between them that she loved frilly, sexy underwear and that he loved to buy it for her, even though he never would let her keep it on long enough to model it for him. She stood in front of the full-length closet mirror in her coral bra and panties, thinking how odd it was undressing and hanging up her clothes at home, and feeling like a stranger. Kay sighed as she removed her underwear and slipped on a simple white cotton nightgown, specifically picking one that Alan hadn't bought for her. Then, still feeling a bit wobbly, she climbed into their big bed under the bay windows and pulled the covers up to her chin.

"How're you doing?" Alan stuck his head around the partly open door and she noticed with surprise that he was blushing. He'd waited to make sure that he wouldn't walk in on her while she was undressing.

"Great. I feel much better. I think I'll be able to sleep tonight." She smiled, thinking what a complete shame it was that she and the gorgeous man bringing a steaming mug of milk over to the bed right now had to be so far apart on so many issues.

"Drink it all," he counseled, sitting beside her. She could feel the muscles of his thigh brush her leg under the covers, and a new weakness overcame her. It was impossible for the two of them to be in physical proximity and not respond passionately to one another. He felt it too and subtly edged away so that they were no longer touching.

"Have to be up kind of early," he told her, watching her sip the drink with the concern and attention of a worried parent. "But sleep in if you like and take the bus later. I won't disturb you." He got up to leave, but she grabbed his hand, nearly upsetting the milk all over the antique quilt.

"Stay with me awhile," she asked. "Just till I get drowsy."

"Sure." He took the cup from her and set it on the bureau by the far wall. Then he walked around the bed, kicking off his shoes as he went. He stretched out his long, agile body on the opposite side of their big bed. He seemed so far away, Kay thought, even though they were only a few feet apart.

Alan crossed his legs and stared up at the ceiling. "I didn't mean to get all crazy about you and that guy, Kay. I just hated him on sight. You understand?"

"I do. I guess it's better that you did see him. I don't want us to have any secrets from each other anymore," she whispered.

He rolled over on one elbow, gazing at her thoughtfully from his respectful distance. "I thought you said the mystery was what made it interesting. What kept a marriage fresh."

"Mystery isn't secrets, Alan. Mysteries can be shared—you can go after the clues together." She reached over and snapped off the bedside lamp. The room was suffused with a yellow-gold light, shed by the full moon hanging above them.

"Go to sleep now," he said softly. "I won't go until you do."

They lay side by side in the darkness, both of them wide-awake and very much aware of each other. For a full quarter of an hour neither of them said a word, yet they could sense each other's smallest thought and most insignificant gesture.

Kay's mind whirled with ideas and feelings and an overwhelming desire that refused to let her lie still. She could feel the blood pulsing in her veins, sense the quiet demands that love made on her. Alan seemed so still on the other side of the bed. Was he asleep?

She reached out one hand at the same instant he did. Their fingers interlocked and held tightly. Neither one could speak, so filled were they with longing and a need to break down the last barrier between them.

Alan moved first, bringing their two hands up over the headboard as he pressed close to her. She could feel the insistent urges of his body through the covers and his clothing, and she moaned as his mouth came down on hers. His hands were everywhere at once, lifting the quilt and pulling aside the sheet. He caressed her slender legs with a sigh of pleasure, and his free hand worked its way under the flimsy nightgown, nearly ripping it. She helped him then, drawing it over her head, leaving herself naked to his view.

He lifted himself up to gaze at her, and the expression on his face told her all she needed to know. She grasped at his belt and undid the buckle as he shrugged off his shirt. Then, not even able to wait until he was fully undressed, he pulled her over on top of him, cupping her breast and bringing it to his mouth. She ached to wrap herself around him, to make them one at once, but he wouldn't allow her to rush. Slowly his mouth and tongue worked their magic on one nipple; then they traced a downward path, moving over her stomach, then up the other side. She entwined her fingers in his curly dark hair and kissed the top of his head, then gently licked the small scar above his left eye.

"Don't hold back from me," Alan breathed in her ear. "Never again."

They wrestled for a moment with his remaining clothes, tossing the covers off the bed. Then there were just the two of them and the moonlight and the ecstasy each gave the other. Kay felt her body filling with new strength now. There was nothing she could not do. Her lover's touch gave her powers she'd never known she possessed, and as she moved over him, kissing and licking first his broad chest with its cloak of silver-tipped curls, then his muscular arms and shoulders, and then the protruding bones of his smooth, tapered hips, she knew that there was no future for her without this man. Together they forged a union that protected them from hate and fear and even tragedy. They had known grief, but never dealt with it as a couple. Now they could deal with their pain and move on.

Alan's large hands enfolded her waist, drawing her closer. He massaged her back until she was loose and pliant in his arms, and then he settled her down over him, easy as a boat slipping into water. Her breath escaped her in an exclamation of joy and wonder and for a second she remained there unmoving, with him as the focus of her entire being.

At last she moved above him, circling and swaying to a music the two of them created. His face showed a range of emotion from caring to laughing to fierce ardor for the woman he cherished. He sat up and clutched her to his chest, then turned them both so deftly that they didn't lose the rhythm of their wild dance. He lay over her, kissing her eyelids and ears, whispering that he would never let her go, that she was his and always would be.

"Kay," he sighed, bringing her to a peak of excitement she had never reached before. "I love you. God, how I love you!"

The meaning of his words sank in slowly. She had been waiting to hear them for so long that at first she wasn't sure. But his eyes spoke eloquently, assuring her that he had never stopped loving her. Even after Sean's death, when she felt she had nothing left inside her to give him, even after she'd run away to Golden, even when he saw her in another man's arms, he had always loved her. And if she had ever doubted that he could care for this new Kay, or that he wouldn't stand for her procrastination and reticence another instant, the expression in his eyes told her that she'd been wrong. Because what they had together was too wonderful and too precious to lose.

"I love you, Alan," she cried out just at the moment when the floodgates of her passion opened and she sobbed her joy in his ear. He joined her and they rode the crest of the wave together.

She could feel his limbs tremble as he eased her back onto the pillows. She stroked his forehead and shoulders, still gasping for breath. They held each other in a close embrace, daring the moment to end. It seemed that time had stopped and that a whole new universe had opened before them.

Grabbing the sheet up from the floor, Alan pulled it over them and they lay sprawled together, facing the open windows. It was very late—or very early—but neither of them cared.

They didn't have to mention the step they were taking. They both knew that the final barrier between them had been smashed, and that now they could take up their life together again. Not that it would mean taking up where they had left off. How could it? Everything had changed, including them and their feelings for each other. But they were nearly all changes for the better. Their marriage might be less perfect and less rosy, but it would surely be more substantial, based on the depths, as well as the heights, of their love for each other.

"Know what I'd like to do sometime this summer?" Kay said just before she drifted off to sleep.

"Ask and it's yours," Alan assured her with a hug.

"Let's take off a weekend and drive up to the Homestead Inn at Big Sur. We had a date to go there a while ago, as I recall," she added shyly.

"Sounds lovely, wife. Now, get some sleep."

"Okay, husband."

Kay snuggled in closer and laid her head on Alan's chest, her ash-blond hair spilling lightly over the pillow. He sighed happily once, then closed his eyes, and when she looked over at him a minute later she could feel the regular, easy breathing that told her he was already asleep.

"I love you," she repeated to his peaceful face. Then she let go of every thought and drifted off into a blissful, restful sleep.

Chapter Thirteen

Being back together was easy now; it was remembering not to be overly protective of each other that was difficult. For Kay there was nothing so wonderful as waking up to the sound of birdsong outside her window and watching the patterns of sunlight shift across her sleeping husband's face. She had never slept much past dawn, anyway, so she had a full hour to take in the wonder of this man she now shared everything with—the laughs, the grumbles, the sorrow and the joy.

The following month, on the anniversary of Sean's death, they sat quietly on the back deck and looked at the stars after dinner. Their tragedy was no longer an ugly little secret, but something they both discussed freely. It was good to reminisce about him that night, but they didn't spend long doing it. His presence in their lives was just as vibrant as ever—only his hovering ghost had vanished like a gust of air.

After that July night they scarcely had a moment free for sitting around. Alan became chairman of his department at the Academy, with a commensurate increase in salary and prestige. Instead of their planned weekend at the Homestead Inn, Kay and Alan ended up traveling to Majorca for an international astronomy convention. By the time they got back a letter was waiting for Kay announcing that the results of her study had been accepted for publication.

"Too much good luck at once," Kay commented, sticking the piece of paper back in its envelope. "I don't trust it."

"Pessimist," Alan taunted her. "We deserve a run of good luck. My theory is that it's infectious, like measles. One of us starts doing well, and the other catches it. Which just goes to show how much of a team we are."

And they were, too. As the months passed Kay felt them growing into a new relationship, unlike the one they'd had before. This wasn't like starting up a marriage again, it was more like rebirth, as though their real personalities hadn't yet come to the fore in their first years together, as if perhaps it had taken a tragedy to bring them out.

Erica was the one who saw it most clearly, probably because the two sisters were so fond of each other. "I don't know," she commented one mid-September day when they were sitting in the kitchen of her new apartment, shelling peas. "I was so dumb before Mark put this gorgeous ring on my finger that I couldn't see what the difference was between living together and marriage."

"Yes?" Kay questioned, popping a few peas into her mouth. "You tell me, sis."

"When you're living together," Erica began slowly, "you notice things about the other person that aren't like you, and you try to iron out differences to make 'you' and 'me' into 'us.' But when you're married the 'us' is taken for granted. All the legal garbage tying you together probably promotes the feeling, but you're really a joint unit, you know? It's the people who fight that kind of togetherness who get themselves into trouble. Like you," she offered.

"What do you mean?" Kay asked suspiciously.

"Well, you can't deny it. Before you came back from Golden you thought of yourself as on your own. You fought Alan every step of the way about getting back together because, deep down, you thought it was a loving gesture to take all the burden off his shoulders. Actually, if you want to look at it closely—which I don't, but I will, for the sake of this conversation—I was the same about Mark. I kept saying, hey, no problem, he wants to live in Minnesota while I have his baby in San Francisco—that's cool. But he was the grown-up. He knew our marriage would change all that detached, laid-back junk."

"Why, Erica," Kay said, coming over to hug her very pregnant sister, "I do believe you're turning conservative on me."

Erica looked up in horror, brandishing the bowl

of peas at her sister. "Don't you even think that!" she hollered.

The baby was born exactly one week later. Mark called Kay and Alan at ten P.M. to announce that they'd just arrived at the hospital.

"I'm going nuts, but I have to be calm," Mark said to them. "You'll never guess what Erica did. She had this sweatshirt printed up that says 'Coach' on it and packed it in her hospital bag with a whistle on a lanyard and a baseball cap. So here I am running around the hospital like a nutty high-school football coach. And I'm going to have a baby! I'm an actor, a juggler—what do I know about fathering?"

Alan and Kay were laughing so hard that it was difficult for them to give Mark a sympathetic answer.

"Listen, I did it, pal," said Alan, who had become very fond of his new brother-in-law. "And you've got a lot more on the ball—after all, you took the classes twice."

"Twice is not enough!" Mark yelled into the phone. "I've got to get back to her."

"We'll be right over," Kay promised as Mark's receiver clattered down.

"I can't believe that girl," Alan said on their way to the hospital a few minutes later. "How could her director even let her go onstage tonight, with the baby due at any minute?"

"Listen, she got them to rewrite the part for a pregnant woman." Kay shrugged, snuggling closer to Alan on the seat as he drove through the silent streets. "If she could do that, she can do anything."

They stayed at the hospital throughout the night. Baby Amanda was born promptly at five A.M., healthy and red and squalling her lungs out. "She's going to be a soprano!" Erica cooed joyfully, looking up at her exhausted husband and her beaming sister and brother-in-law, who had crowded into her room as soon as they were allowed.

They debated about going home to sleep, but Mark wasn't about to leave his family, so Kay and Alan went out to breakfast. At seven they called Katherine in Golden and then ran around town all day, picking up little things they were sure Erica and Mark had never thought to buy. By the time they got back to the hospital it was six P.M. Erica was rested and sitting up in bed, with her baby beside her.

"I can't believe it," Erica said when Kay and Alan walked in. "Can you believe it? She's real—all her fingers and toes and her tiny heartbeat! I love her—isn't that weird? I've only known her for a few hours and I'm nuts about her."

"That's called motherhood." Kay laughed. "No one can resist the feeling."

"Well . . . ?" Erica grinned. "Don't keep me in suspense. How'd I do?"

"I give it a rave review." Alan let one finger caress the baby's soft downy head.

"Oh, you mean the show!" Kay said. "I'd say you deserve an award from what I hear. Going onstage was incredible enough, but finishing the performance just as you were going into labor . . . I wish I'd seen it," Kay marveled, carefully watching Alan watching the baby.

"Little Amanda here is a natural," Erica declared. "She knew every one of her cues. I only wish she'd waited a few more minutes so I could have made the curtain call." She sighed.

"Now, there's an inveterate actress talking," Alan marveled. "Greedy for applause to the end."

"Hey, mister," Erica corrected him, "this is the beginning."

"I know that." The three of them were quiet for a moment as Amanda stirred and gurgled in her sleep. She was so small, so delicate, Kay thought. She had such a life ahead of her.

"I wouldn't worry about that curtain call," Alan said. "Now you've got a captive audience of one."

"That's true. Kay, did you tell Mom to get on the next plane out of Colorado?" Erica began fussing with Amanda's blanket, and the baby let out a big burp.

"I couldn't have stopped her." Kay laughed. "But I have to warn you, she was really annoyed at us. At you for delivering before she got here—*and* in the middle of the night to boot—and at me and Mark for not calling the instant it occurred so she could at least have been with you in spirit. Alan's the only one she's not furious with."

"Well, that's always been true." Alan smiled, wrapping his arms around his wife's waist. "If she hadn't been cheering for me all those months, Kay might never have come around."

"Oh, Alan, she would too," Erica declared. "Kay's just stubborn. You have to beat her into submission occasionally. Don't you know that yet?"

"Uh-uh." Alan grinned and kissed his wife. "She

can do whatever she wants and be as stubborn as she likes—as long as I'm included."

Kay and Alan kissed lightly and Erica harrumphed, clearly expecting that she and her new baby should be the center of attention. "All right, lovebirds, cut it out. So how does Mom like Amanda Katherine Sabia as a name? That mellowed her out, I bet."

"Sorry, sis." Kay reluctantly extricated herself from Alan's arms. "You can't win with her. She couldn't understand why it wasn't Katherine Amanda Sabia!"

"Oh, boy!" Erica giggled. "I know her visit's going to be a doozy. Meeting my new child and my new husband all at once. Let's not remind her that she couldn't come to the wedding because we—shall we say?—eloped. Do people still say that?" Erica frowned.

"I think they do." Alan bent over the hospital bed and scooped up Amanda with all her blankets for a better look. "She's gorgeous, kid, no doubt about it. Now, any advice Mark wants—or doesn't want—on fathering, I'll be delighted to supply. I'm an old hand."

"Where is that husband of yours, by the way?" Kay demanded. She couldn't take her eyes off Alan, so much did the picture of man and child remind her of another day, another birth. But it was all right now—she loved the sight of him so tender, so caring.

"Gee, that's a good question," Erica said, reaching for her baby. "He was here twenty minutes ago and then he vanished. Said he had to get something." She shook her head, smiling. "I think this whole experience went to his head. He used to tell me he adored kids, wanted to have a passel of them to make up for being an only child, but the reality of it is something else again. Probably went to get himself some laughing gas. I mean, I would if I were a father."

Alan gave her a quizzical look. "You think being the father is harder?"

"Oh, definitely." She lounged back on her pillows and struck a theatrical pose with her baby in her arms. "See, when you're the mother everyone makes a big fuss, tells you how great you are, how well you got through labor, how you look positively glowing. And you can *see* what you did. But the man . . ." She shrugged. "He generally looks green from worry. He can't *do* anything but rush around and massage his wife and hold his kid. He doesn't feel he's accomplished anything."

Alan looked hard at Kay, and although he was answering Erica, it was clear that he was talking directly to Kay. "Not true. He's accomplished a hell of a lot. He's a different person for being a father. It turns his head around. And his heart. Because now he's head over heels in love with two people at the same time—his wife and his child. He has so done something, and his feelings are tangible proof."

Erica and Kay were quiet, taking in what he'd just said. Kay was filled with a mix of emotions, listening to this man who had known the same heartache she had. He really had come out on top of it. Probably, in private, he'd confess to new worries—with new life, there were always new worries. But she knew that it would be a mistake to think only of the dark side. Right now, at this moment, the only important thing was the promise of the future—for Amanda and for all of them.

The door swung open and they turned to see Mark, gasping and panting, race to his family's bedside.

"I'm sorry, sweetheart. It took longer than I thought."

Erica gave Kay a sly wink. "I'm not even going to ask him what was so urgent."

"I needed these." Mark pulled a new can of tennis balls from his jacket pocket and ripped off the top. He spilled the three yellow balls out into his hand and began to juggle them as a large, peaceful smile spread across his face.

"I hate to tell you this, ole buddy," Alan offered, "but your daughter hasn't even opened her eyes yet. She's not getting much out of this."

"Oh, I know that." Mark grinned, flipping one ball over his head and a second behind his back.

"This is therapy, folks." Erica sighed. "For him."

"See, I'm on such a high because of my two beautiful girls that I've got to burn off some energy. This is my own surefire method."

Everyone had a good laugh except for Amanda, awakened by all the commotion, who began to cry loudly and continuously.

"Uh-oh." Kay took Alan's arm as the new mother and father tried to comfort their infant. "Let's get out of here for a while so they can get some peace and quiet. We'll be back later, okay?"

But Erica and Mark were oblivious of everything

except Amanda. Kay and Alan were out the door before they knew it.

"I'm pooped." He yawned and stretched. "Did we get any sleep last night?"

"You did," Kay said wryly. "I watched you."

"Yeah, big talker. You're the best sleeper on the West Coast. Even if you don't eat much breakfast these days, I would say you're definitely in training to be a hedonist." He kissed her lightly as they walked down the hospital steps into the clear evening.

"Well, it's Sunday night, a lazy time." Kay grinned mischievously. "Perfect for lying around and doing nothing. Come on, I'll race you to the car."

She had never felt so hopeful, so completely at ease with herself. In the months that she had been back together with Alan, they had in effect rededicated themselves to making each other happy. She could talk about her feelings now—maybe because she had more of them to talk about. And especially today, of all days, she was light-headed with news, ready to crow with delight. She could hardly wait.

They found the Sunday paper waiting on the top porch step and Alan carried it out to the back deck while Kay fixed some herb tea. There was a chill in the air, and the bay glistened with starlight, little white peaks dancing on the water alongside the boats docked at the Sausalito landing.

Kay brought the tea out and walked over to join her husband, who was quietly surveying the sky. There was a faraway look on his handsome face that Kay hadn't seen there for a while. She knew that he was thinking about Sean.

"It's funny, isn't it?" she murmured, slipping her arm through his. "My baby sister with a baby. I still can't get over it."

"Makes you feel sort of old, doesn't it?" Alan mused. "I always thought of uncles as older, fat and jolly, and always ready with a piece of advice."

"You don't fit the picture." Kay frowned. "No, I can't say you'll make it as an uncle. Or me as an aunt, baking pies and yelling about muddy shoes on the carpet."

"Uh-uh." He looked at her appraisingly. "You don't fit the bill as an aunt. Too sexy." He clasped his hands behind her head and drew her close for a kiss, parting her lips with his tongue.

"You taste good." Kay sighed, wrapping her arms around him. "I think I'll skip dinner and concentrate on you." They stood by the railing in a close embrace for a long moment. Kay's heart was pounding as she pulled away. It was crucial, especially tonight, that she not hold back on her husband. "I have something to tell you."

"Can't it wait?" He reached for her, but she shook her head and walked a few steps away.

"Just a second. I have to say this. You know, I don't feel older because of Amanda. Younger, if anything. How can I put it? I feel connected, more responsible—even more than I did when Sean was born."

"Oh?" He had that nervous look on his face, as though he was afraid that the mention of their dead child might be too much for her, but she smiled, assuring him.

"I used to be so independent—separate from

everything and everyone, the tough-minded, iron-willed scientist."

"I remember." He nodded.

"For all Erica says about marriage being so different from living together, well, that never hit me. Back then, we hadn't changed enough, you see? We were still essentially the same people as when we were single. And we kept it up—I know I did. And when Sean was born I wanted to hoard him, keep him separate, too, just for us. I wasn't ready to be a mother then, I don't think."

Alan looked at her in amazement. He'd never heard her be so honest before, especially about Sean.

"With Amanda around, though," Kay went on, "it's all so different. I guess because of what we've been through. I feel like an important part of a family now. Like when I was a kid, and we lived on Elkin Street, and Dad was alive and on holidays there'd be all those cousins—"

"And aunts and uncles," Alan pointed out, coming to her.

"Exactly. People I could turn to, talk to, share things with. Now there's someone in the world who may look to me for help and advice someday. That changes your whole perspective."

He took her hand and their fingers linked tightly. "I don't know if you're saying that's good or bad."

"Neither." She shook her head. "Just different. I guess I like the new me. Do you?" she asked earnestly, burning to tell him and unsure of how to do it.

"Yes. She surprises me sometimes. All the

time," he admitted. "But I do like her. I love you," he murmured.

Kay melted closer, leaning her head on his shoulder. Those words were so precious to her, and every time he said them, they meant more.

"Look!" Kay jerked away, pointing to the sky where a falling star streaked across the night, its brilliant tail scoring the heavens.

Alan pulled her close, resting his chin on her soft hair, his arms around her waist as they silently watched the spectacle.

"'Twinkle, twinkle, little star,'" Alan recited wistfully. "'How I wonder where you are . . .'"

Kay turned slightly in his arms and gently outlined his strong features with a finger. "What are you thinking?" she whispered.

"About shooting stars. A dying star burning itself out. Wouldn't it be strange if that were Sean's spirit fading away, now that Amanda has come to take its place? Not that I'm superstitious, of course." He laughed awkwardly. "I'd get drummed out of the Academy for a statement like that."

"I'll never tell." Kay smiled. "But that particular shooting star was a new spirit on its way to earth."

"And how do you know that?" he asked suspiciously. "You're a biologist."

"A good one, too." She nodded, certain now that the time was right for them. "This woman's intuition I've got, though, it's pretty strong tonight. And it tells me that that star was a brand-new little one about to come into the world."

He moved her away from him and gazed deep

into her glinting green eyes. "I take it you're not formulating a new theory. This is just a hunch?"

"Not a theory. A fact." She leaned in close and kissed him, willing him to know what it was she was about to say. Their hearts and minds were nearly touching.

"Do you know who that new spirit is, Alan? Have you any idea?"

His face was a mask of confusion and she could tell that he was about to accuse her of toying with him, of letting him dare to believe. She let him work it out for a moment and then, just as an expression of startled recognition crossed his face, she took both his hands and laid them flat on her stomach. "I think that new spirit is with us already, my darling," she whispered.

Alan was speechless, but his eyes devoured her. His face floated before her in the pale moonlight, filled with both wonder and terror. He was afraid to voice the words, amazed that they could really be true.

"I'm pregnant." Kay nodded. "Truth."

He pressed her against him with a sob of joy and she could feel his heart beating like a wild bird in his chest. "I love you so much, Kay." His mouth found hers and he kissed her deeply, fondly, more tender than she'd ever remembered him being. Then the kisses grew more passionate and they clutched each other, needing the pressure of hands and lips and limbs to reinforce the reality of this precious moment. They were going to have a child.

"When did you know?" he asked.

"I'm not sure. Maybe only tonight, after I saw

Amanda. I wasn't watching the signs too carefully until then."

Alan laughed. "I've been watching. Like a hawk."

"And do you agree?" she asked.

"I do. And I'm thrilled. I could sing."

"No." She put a hand over his mouth before he could open it. "This won't be a cinch, you know. We're bound to worry a little."

He took her by the hand and ushered her through the sliding glass doors that led from the deck to the living room. The pot of tea, now stone cold, sat like a stolid little lamp on the table, waiting for a genie to jump out of it.

"Leave the worrying to me this time," Alan suggested, drawing his wife down the corridor to the bedroom.

"No, this time we'll handle it together."

He walked her backward to the big bed, wrapping her in his muscular embrace. With a sigh of delight that was almost too soft to be heard, he said, "I want you, Kay. More than ever." He rained kisses on her neck and throat until she was forced to lie back on the mattress, opening her arms to her lover, her husband, her alter ego.

Under the beaming moon they made love with an intensity and passion that only two people who had traveled the same roads together could create. In the distance the sound of a foghorn on the bay reminded them that they were still on earth, in their house, protected by their love. But they felt that they might have been a million light-years away, because nothing existed for them during that long night of desire and romance except each other.

Now Kay knew that she had finally healed. The hurt and sense of loss she had carried with her for a year dropped away like a heavy anchor, sinking to the bottom of the sea. And she rose, freeing herself from its weight and from the sense of loss that had clung to her so persistently. This was the mystery—how a woman could know a man this well and yet have only just discovered him.

Alan kissed her softly, his lips leaving a burning trail from one end of her body to the other. "To have and to hold," he whispered in her ear. "For better or for worse, for richer or for poorer." The last line remained unspoken as he entered her, filling her with ecstasy.

But death could not part them now; they both knew that. Their marriage, their love, had been reborn in their hearts, and together they were ready to meet whatever their futures held. They had everything now, because they had hope.

Silhouette Special Edition. Romances for the woman who expects a little more out of love.

If you enjoyed this book, and you're ready for more great romance

...get 4 romance novels FREE when you become a Silhouette Special Edition home subscriber.

Act now and we'll send you four exciting Silhouette Special Edition romance novels. They're our gift to introduce you to our convenient home subscription service. Every month, we'll send you six new passion-filled Special Edition books. Look them over for 15 days. If you keep them, pay just $11.70 for all six. Or return them at no charge.

We'll mail your books to you two full months *before they are available anywhere else.* Plus, with every shipment, you'll receive the Silhouette Books Newsletter absolutely free. *And with Silhouette Special Edition there are never any shipping or handling charges.*

Mail the coupon today to get your four free books—and more romance than you ever bargained for.

MAIL COUPON TODAY

Silhouette Special Edition®
120 Brighton Road, P.O. Box 5020, Clifton, N. J. 07015

☐ Yes, please send me FREE and without obligation, 4 exciting Silhouette Special Edition romance novels. Unless you hear from me after I receive my 4 FREE BOOKS, please send me 6 new books to preview each month. I understand that you will bill me just $1.95 each for a total of $11.70—with no additional shipping, handling or other charges. **There is no minimum number of books that I must buy, and I can cancel anytime I wish.** The first 4 books are mine to keep, even if I never take a single additional book.

☐ Mrs. ☐ Miss ☐ Ms. ☐ Mr. **BSS1R4**

Name (please print)

Address Apt. No.

City State Zip

Signature (If under 18, parent or guardian must sign.)

This offer, limited to one per customer, expires July 31, 1984. Terms and prices subject to change. Your enrollment is subject to acceptance by Simon & Schuster Enterprises.